The
Fourth Stage of
Gainsborough
Brown

The Fourth Stage of Gainsborough Brown

by
*Clarissa
Watson*

M W SUSPENSE

David McKay Company, Inc.
Ives Washburn, Inc.
New York

Library of Congress Cataloging in Publication Data

Watson, Clarissa.
The fourth stage of Gainsborough Brown.

(MW suspense)
I. Title.

PZ4.W3386Fo   [PS3573.A848]   813'.5'4   76-45651
ISBN 0-679-50667-5

MANUFACTURED IN THE UNITED STATES OF AMERICA

10 9 8 7 6 5 4 3 2 1

For Berenice,
who could not wait

Prologue

I can paint you a picture of Gainsborough Brown more accurately with a brush than I can with words—in fact, I have painted him. It's the portrait you see over and over again every time the story is dredged up in connection with an exhibition of his pictures. And each time it appears in some publication, a rash of requests for sittings follows; and I have to explain all over again that I am a painter, not a portrait artist, and that I only happened to do Gainsborough Brown because he was an interesting subject. My official stance is that something about him appealed to me, as one artist to another—which, at the time I did the picture, was more or less true.

I painted Gainsborough Brown when I was just beginning to know him, and I still remember what a struggle it was. There was something about him—a malicious ill will, I suppose—that defied me when I tried to imprison it on canvas. In the end I had to resort to dozens of quick pencil sketches before I found the attitude I wanted. Happily, I am the complete master of my pencil. In seconds it will catch the essence of a motion, the accurate impression of a landscape, the characteristic tilt of a head. And my artist's eye is my pencil's servant, endlessly at work storing away images and impressions, none too neatly but accurately enough so they can be brought out and transferred to paper months and even years later with the freshness of a sight just seen.

As a matter of fact, if it weren't for that combination of artist's skill and memory, the Persis Willum portrait of a brooding Gainsborough Brown—forever after described by the press with its usual hindsight as a portrait of a man "marked for tragedy"—would have been my major contribution to *l'affaire* Gainsborough.

Gainsborough Brown was famous as a painter, of course. He was also a number of other things before he discovered this interesting fact about himself. He was a boy who never finished school and never read a book, and later a man who let his young wife support him while he kicked around from one job to another, none of them ever "good enough" for him. We knew this much because he told us. And we never questioned that a young woman would be willing to work to support him because we could see for ourselves that his dark and glowering good looks generally exercised a kind of Heathcliff magic on women, who often found him irresistible, as later events were to prove.

He was also a hypochondriac, a malingerer and a bully— we learned this as we grew to know him. And he had a most stupendous ego—so stupendous that he seemed to keep his life before he became an artist as secret as possible so that the world might think of him as having emerged full and complete and dazzling from the brow of Zeus or some other deity equally suited to the honor. Naturally, no matter how much he may have desired it for the sake of his public image, his origins were less than mythical. Gregor Olitsky, who didn't appear on the scene until the Second Stage, used to say that Gainsborough Brown had emerged in three stages.

The First Stage was after he had painted his first few pictures. They had attracted attention when his canvases and mine hung side by side in an obscure and unfashionable gallery downtown. An undistinguished little warren, it was the kind of gallery that subsists on the "hanging fees" paid by the artists, all of whom were too poor, too unknown or too lacking in talent to warrant wall space uptown.

The gallery had offered to forswear the hanging fee in my case—galleries like this usually did even though, as a painter, I had a long way to go before the uptown galleries would consider me. This courtesy was offered on the theory that my name, as the niece of a famous collector, would lend the exhibition a little bit of cachet. The hope was also that Aunt Lydie herself would come to see the show and perhaps part with a little of her money in the process. I always insisted on paying the fee and I never sent my aunt an invitation. She understood why.

There was an arresting quality about Gains's work in those days which caught my eye, and he himself was so unkempt and forbidding that I thought he could use some help, if only for the sake of the young wife he said was toiling away back home. Furthermore, he was out of a job. So I began to peddle his work among Aunt Lydie's friends, and in a very short time he achieved a minor vogue among them. (I was less high-principled about using my connections on someone else's behalf.)

He was signing his pictures just plain "Brown" then; and later, when I was able to persuade him that there were too many just plain *Browns* in the world, O. G. Brown. The "O," I discovered, stood for "Oscar," and you may be sure he made a pact with me instantly that the dreaded word should never pass either of our lips. Like Monet, he'd known all the time that there was no glamour in "Oscar." And no one in the art world ever knew the truth. The name never appeared in print as long as he lived or after he died. If anyone ever asked about the big, round "O," we both said it was for "Ogden," a name he picked out of the social register and thus considered worthy.

From the beginning he thought in dramatic terms. He referred to me as his "discoverer" and "mentor" and to himself as "humble" and "honored" and "unworthy." He also thought in practical terms, never forgetting my relationship to Aunt Lydie. I learned much later that he had paid an extra fee to have his work hung next to mine in that first show.

In the Second Stage he became O. Gainsborough Brown. He also became a year younger in his catalogue and publicity, a habit he was to follow pretty regularly from then on. I never knew whether the mysterious middle "G" actually stood for Gainsborough or whether, when Gregor Olitsky took over Gains's career, Gregor produced the Gainsborough—it had the Olitsky touch.

Gregor discovered Gains's work when attending a dinner party at the house of a friend of Aunt Lydie's. There were two small Browns hanging in the hallway, and they were just different enough to catch Gregor's attention. One has to remember that the art world was on an abstract kick at that time, and it took about two minutes for Gregor to equate the new look of magnified realism in Gainsborough Brown's work with a hunch that the fashion pendulum in art was bound to swing back. Within a week he had found Gains and signed him to a six-year contract. That was a long time as contracts go. But Gains was glad to get it.

Now Gregor became the "discoverer." And this time the word was appropriate, because O. Gainsborough Brown improved and prospered in the chain of chic galleries which Gregor operated wherever the very rich congregated—in Palm Beach, Nantucket, Palm Springs and Long Island's North Shore. The art magazines, the newspapers and particularly the society columns gave generous coverage to the artist and his activities as Gregor placed his work in more and more good collections. The quality of Gains's work improved, and Gregor even managed to get him into a few national shows. During the Second Stage Gains announced rather disinterestedly that his wife had divorced him and run off with another man; the announcement was not exactly earthshaking, for none of us had ever laid eyes on her. Meanwhile, his conversation had a single theme: "my talent," "my talent," "my talent." His vocabulary wasn't expanding, but his sense of his own importance was already almost out of bounds.

The Third Stage, assisted by Gregor's genius as a promoter, is the one with which most people are familiar through the PBS series, the award-winning documentary and the elaborate catalogues for the Los Angeles and MOMA shows. This was the stage of plain Gainsborough Brown, the Great American Contemporary, True Portrayer of America Today, now discovered by Lydie Wentworth, the great American collector. How Aunt Lydie hated *that;* but as long as Gains was alive to speak to the press and Gregor encouraged him, there wasn't much she could do to deny it without seeming ungracious. She did demur at first, but so gracefully that the press would say, "Railroad heiress Miss Wentworth, with her usual modesty, denied that she had been in any way instrumental in the career of the painter; but it is a well-known fact that this discerning collector etc. etc."

Aunt Lydie once complained rather pathetically, "I don't understand. The more I say I had nothing to do with making that young man famous, the more they write about me. I don't even own one of his pictures—I think they're ugly—but I can't very well say so, can I?" I still recall Gregor's cheerful reply. "Never mind, Lydia. Any minute now Gainsborough Brown will announce that he was actually discovered by God. Then we can all relax."

By now Gains was making a great deal of money and parting with it as fast as he could. Most of his time was spent in Europe, staying at the fine hotels and indulging himself in what he called the "high life" (he had a penchant for antique phrases). It had become increasingly difficult to persuade him to paint enough for the annual one-man shows his contract called for, and at the end he was asking Gregor for advances on paintings yet unpainted.

Shortly after his divorce, he acquired a secretary to tend to his affairs. She was a mousy, bespectacled woman named Miss Ives, who appeared to live in terror of offending Gainsborough and who soon became prey to constant headaches brought on, no doubt, by her employer's foul disposition. Her one ambition seemed to be to sink into the woodwork and disappear. We did our best to make her happy by ignoring her.

It was at the very end of the Third Stage that Gainsborough brought home a new wife—a nice young woman called Alida, whom he had met in Paris. We heard that she was supposed to be rich . . . that she had come with her own French chauffeur. But we barely got to know her.

Then there was a Fourth Stage of Gainsborough Brown, the stage Gregor hadn't anticipated—the *now* stage, the one in which Gainsborough Brown is dead, "cut off cruelly at the peak of his talents," to quote from a particularly nauseating article. Dead of drowning in the middle of a gala party, where he was mingling with the members of fashionable society—a victim, according to fast-growing legend, of the exhaustion of preparing for a new exhibition combined with a misstep into an unlighted swimming pool and topped off by a lamentable inability to swim a single stroke. Dead, moreover, on a national holiday and in full costume, details which Gains himself couldn't have planned more perfectly to please the press.

He is buried, but his story is very much alive. The networks are taping interviews for more specials. Museums as far away as Rotterdam are negotiating for retrospectives. Three paperback publishers—one of them French—have rushed books into print. There is even a rumor that a number of prominent painters are working on canvases entitled *Death of an Artist* for the winter exhibitions.

Gains would have been very gratified to know that he was the center of all this excitement, the protagonist of a story which mixed art, society and violent death in a marvelous potpourri designed to make a myth of a man. Certainly, it would have made a celebrity out of any corpse.

Yes, the story was perfect. The story was too perfect.

The

Fourth Stage of

Gainsborough

Brown

The first word of the party at which Gainsborough Brown was to die came one day in late spring when Aunt Lydie and I were having one of our rare lunches in town together.

I was late. First of all, I was coming in from Long Island and the train was late. Usually we saw each other on weekends, which she spent at her place, The Crossing, in the country. It was called The Crossing because it occupied most of the land between two of the major roads that originally crossed the North Shore of Long Island, an amount of acreage staggering to contemplate.

I was also late because it was raining; and, as everyone knows, it is impossible to get around in New York when it rains. After I finally emerged from the bowels of the Long Island Railroad station, I had to practically lie down in the middle of Eighth Avenue to stop a cab.

Aunt Lydie had already ordered her lunch when I arrived. She didn't have to contend with such boring trivialities as trains and cabs ... she stayed at her Park Avenue apartment during the week and was transported punctually to all of her appointments by limousine.

She didn't bother to say "hello" to me. "I do wish Giovanni would be all on one floor," she said, as if we had been discussing the matter for some time. "Very soon now I shall be at an age where I may find stairs tiring, and I should hate to have to stop coming here. But then I suppose if he did do something about it the restaurant would never be the same, and I do hate to see things change."

My aunt was in particularly good form; if she would soon be taxed by the problems of climbing stairs, it certainly didn't show. Part of the credit, of course, belonged to her multi-talented personal maid, Hannah, who was expert at everything from hairdressing to martini-mixing. And Hannah had seen to it that she was beautifully turned out in a beige Norell. (Aunt Lydie had developed a passion for Norell after Balenciaga died.) Her jewels were spectacular—a necklace of pearls, which seemed as big as a hen's eggs, and a sapphire ring in blazing accord with the sapphires in her earrings, bracelet and pin.

She was, by her own admission, extravagant about jewelry. She didn't wear it; she displayed it. "It's one of my little weaknesses," she would say. "But what good are they in a box or, worse yet, in a vault? My father used to say that he was leaving me a great deal of money and I mustn't waste it. But paintings and jewels were different, he always told me. They were an *investment*. And I like to *see* my investments. As a matter of fact" (this was confided to me once in a whisper), "I was advised during the Cuban missile crisis that the only thing worth taking down into my air-raid shelter was my jewels. Nothing else would be valuable after we all came out again. Just suppose the bombs *had* come and I'd been caught in someone else's air-raid shelter—and I hadn't been wearing any of my jewels! Just think about that for a minute!" I tried and gave up.

Jewelry aside, as I studied the woman across the table from me, I had to admit that Hannah was only partially responsible for the results. She had great material to work with, for my aunt had the wispy figure of a young girl and a cap of silver hair. Her hair had been silver for as long as I could remember, and she wore it in a sort of 1920s "bob" which, on her, gave the impression of immense chic. Beside her I felt like a rain-drenched wreck. Once in a while when I've got it all together, I can look pretty sensational. But I don't have it all together that often, and generally I'm just medium . . . medium blonde, medium tall, medium young, medium everything. Today I was medium sodden, too.

"Do have some of this," my aunt was saying. She gestured toward her plate, and I realized that as a penance for being late I was expected to forswear a cocktail. Then she relented. "You should have a glass of wine with lunch to warm you up."

There was a flurry of activity while I ordered, aided by her interested suggestions. My aunt was always surrounded by those little flurries that every move of the very rich seems to generate and to which they appear totally oblivious. I struggled with the desire to light a cigarette. (I was always resisting a desire to smoke; I was trying to give it up. Furthermore, my aunt was one of the stalwarts who *had* given up smoking, and the mere sight of anyone about to strike a match now sent her into delicate fits of coughing.)

"I never seem to see you any more since you began working for Gregor Olitsky—at least I never seem to see you without him. How long has it been, four years? I mean that you've worked for him at his Long Island gallery?"

"The North Shore Gallery," I supplied automatically.

She went on to the next subject without waiting for my answer to how long it had been (four and a half years exactly). It was typical of her, and it gave many people the impression that she was quixotic. They couldn't have been more mistaken. So I knew there was a message for me somewhere in what she was saying; but before I could fathom it she had changed tack. "I'm thinking of giving myself a little party for my birthday."

A waiter came with my order, and she waited until I was served before she continued.

"Do you think it's awful to give oneself a party? I think it's all right as long as it's a birthday, don't you? I'll call it a Fourth of July party so that people won't think they have to bring presents. I love presents, but it wouldn't be nice to have a party for that reason. Actually, I've always considered myself extremely fortunate to have been born on a national holiday; and this could be a sort of patriotic gesture. Anyway, there may not be too many birthdays left for me to celebrate." She looked at me fiercely. "Don't ask me which birthday it is."

I was not about to. Besides, I knew. She was going to be sixty-five. It didn't seem possible, but it was a fact.

"Gregor and I will still be in Paris then—the annual buying trip," I said instead. It was the one time of year we could get away for more than a few consecutive days. And while I spent most of my time in the Long Island gallery or Gregor's New York office, I actually helped to oversee the entire operation.

"That's all taken care of. I spoke to Gregor on the phone this morning, and he's changing your return flight to the morning of the Fourth. Both of you. He was dear about it. Still, Persis, I do think it looks odd for you to be going off with him like that. He's an extremely attractive man; I believe he's considered something of a catch among the women who know about things like that. I mean, I understand that there are certain women who have been after him for years. Under the circumstances, aren't you afraid people will gossip?"

I felt myself blush with embarrassment. The circumstances were that Gregor was old enough to be my father. But I couldn't very well say so; after all, he was almost exactly Aunt Lydie's age and she wouldn't have liked that. So I explained instead what Aunt Lydie must perfectly well know—that it was purely business; that we stayed on separate floors of the Meurice; that Gregor said he needed me because my French was better than his; that I helped select the paintings Gregor bought; that I kept all the records and attended to Customs and so forth. I must say, explaining it to her that way, it sounded pretty dull, so I tried to defend myself another way.

"After all, I'm thirty-six and I have been married. It's not as if I were some little debutante. And by helping Gregor, I'm also helping a number of talented artists make a good living. It makes me feel useful. And I see a lot of people; if I were staying at home painting, I'd never see anyone. This is better for me."

There was a pause. I suppose both of us were thinking of the man I had once been married to—the man who had taken just ten years to run through my small inheritance and to drink himself to death. I must have loved him once, in the beginning. But I couldn't believe it now.

Aunt Lydie didn't like to think about troubles—any-body's troubles—so her voice was brusque. "Don't you think it's time you tried marriage again? It might be very different this time. Not with someone Gregor's age, but with a young man." (There was a definite emphasis on the "young.") "For example, the one who used to hang around you all the time, you know, the Reynolds boy. He was a very nice young man." There it was again.

I shrugged. "There's no one." It was true. It seemed to me that after the lacerating experience of my first marriage a second attempt would be madness. True, as my aunt said, Oliver Reynolds was nice, but perhaps too much so. I was suspicious of all that niceness. And no wonder—everyone else, with the possible exception of Gregor, who was too old for me and too busy to want to tie himself down in marriage to anyone, seemed interested in me as an ultimate end to my aunt and her famous fortune. I don't honestly think it was my imagination, although it's easy to get complexes when you're around people with as much money as Aunt Lydie. I must have heard of a thousand schemes that would prosper if only she'd make a small investment!

"Well, I still say the right marriage would be good for you. You should be painting more." She peered desperately at her jewel-encrusted wristwatch to keep me from guessing from her expression that concern for my domestic situation was probably the reason we were lunching today. But I knew her too well to be fooled, even though the prospect of Aunt Lydie's recommending marriage struck me as lu-dicrous. No other woman, with the possible exception of

5

good Queen Bess, had so successfully avoided the state of matrimony while not denying herself the gentle pleasures of love. I had been hearing rumors about her love affairs forever without once hearing the mention of a specific name. Apparently her affairs were all slightly misty, of short duration and conducted on a decorous level, if such a thing is possible. One thing was certain: Legions of men may have won her heart for a time, but none had ever won her fortune.

She may have sensed what I was thinking, for she dropped the matter, and we chatted pleasantly about trivialities through the rest of lunch. She adored harmless gossip, and I always stored up what few tidbits I had heard to entertain her with when we met.

As I jabbered on, the little frown lines that had first gathered between her eyebrows with the mention of Gregor disappeared and her mouth lost the petulant look it always had when she forced herself to be serious until finally she was laughing in that unaffectedly exuberant way that always took people by surprise. It wasn't until we were ready to leave and she was carefully sorting out the tip that she dropped her real bombshell. "With the galleries planning to expand and open a Paris branch, I can understand that you would be very interested and involved. But the thing I want to emphasize is that you shouldn't think of Gregor Olitsky in terms of marriage, no matter how attractive he is. Definitely not. It wouldn't do at all." She buried her nose deliberately in her small change. "There are good reasons, which I have no intention of going into. You will just have to take my word."

Before I could even finish forming the thought that she was talking like someone out of a boarding-school play, she stood up and we were engulfed by a regiment of bowing waiters and by Giovanni himself, who loved her and insisted on escorting her down the stairs and right out to the sidewalk, where the favorite of her three chauffeurs, Roberts, waited to help her into her car. I was riding uptown with her as far as the Whitney Museum, where I wanted to see a new exhibition in which Gains had a picture, so I climbed in after her and settled down happily into the deep upholstery of the back seat.

I loved riding with Aunt Lydie. She was at her most beguiling in her stately car. It was always the same. As we glided through the traffic with the dignity of a great passenger ship, she sat with her nose glued to the window, bewitched by the activities of the people on the street, while the people on the street, in turn, craned to see who could be riding by in such a burnished, high-topped, splendidly ancient English motorcar. It was one of her little conceits to say that she could never replace her car because she couldn't remember its name; but I doubted if she would ever have to replace it—Roberts kept it in absolute mint condition.

She didn't mention Gregor again; she was too busy peering through the rain-splashed side window and exclaiming over everything she saw. And since I had no intention of marrying Gregor anyway—nor he me—I decided to chalk up her little speech to pure whimsy. Later I was not so sure.

As we glided sedately up Madison Avenue ("I don't understand why people are always buying new cars. Look how marvelous this one is in traffic!") we both spotted a familiar figure. Even so close to the Whitney, where exotic types abound, Gainsborough Brown was spectacularly noticeable with his wild hair and the black gaucho clothes he was currently affecting. Not only that; he towered over the landscape like a lighthouse, sloshing along oblivious to the rain, his long hair streaming in ribbons along his bony cheeks and his voluminous black britches flapping dankly against his shanks. There was a redheaded girl with him, a tall, long-legged girl who nonetheless was half running to keep up with him. She had the face of a ravished angel—all planes and hollows and suffering and childlike softness mixed together into something lovely. Unforgettable.

As if she felt me looking at her, she glanced past Gains and caught me watching. For what seemed a very long moment our eyes met. Hers were beautiful—even at a distance, even washed with rain. Gains would like that. "A woman's beauty is in her eyes," he would say, fixing you with his own angry dark ones. "Without beautiful eyes she has no beauty." My aunt was trying to peer around me, saying, "Isn't that Gainsborough Brown? Well, naturally it is. No one else could possibly manage to look like that, even by design. And that must be his new wife."

I knew I had to distract her so I dropped my purse on the floor and busied myself picking up the scattered contents until I was sure the car had moved well past the two on the street. Aunt Lydie automatically bent to help me, and by the time we were finished, Gains and his companion were almost out of sight.

"Wasn't it interesting to come upon them like that?" My aunt seemed inordinately pleased to have seen someone she despised as cordially as she did Gains. "I wish I had gotten a look at her. I must remember to ask them to my party. As you know, I do dislike him; but he's the kind of person other people like to meet because he's always in the papers; and one needs a number of those types to make a party successful."

"They've probably been to the exhibition." I didn't know what else to say. "Gains likes to go every single day when he has a picture hanging somewhere. He stands next to it and listens for flattering comments and hopes he'll be recognized. He loves signing catalogues and gets quite cross if he's not noticed."

I was praying she hadn't had a good look at the girl because of my diversionary tactics and the rain. Otherwise she would have a shock when she finally did meet Gains's new bride; and her opinion of him was low enough as it was. I had met the new Mrs. Brown a few days before. And I just didn't have the courage to tell my aunt that, whoever she was, the girl with Gainsborough Brown was definitely not his wife.

8

2

The night of Aunt Lydie's "little" party was so beautiful that everything seemed to take on another dimension. A whole sky full of stars shimmered overhead as if engaged in a contest to outshine the thousands of tiny white, man-made lights strung through the trees and shrubbery on the grounds.

My aunt maintained later that she had only invited six hundred people. If so, eight or nine hundred more must have crashed the party because there were people every-where and the four immense buffets and the dozen bars were inundated. Someone said afterward that if Louis XIV himself had been present, no one would have noted him in the crush.

Intimate groupings of tables and chairs were placed throughout the gardens and lawns, each table with its own little candle. The ways and paths between were lighted by flaming torchères. Two orchestras alternated in the cov-ered, air-conditioned tennis court, and guests who chose to could dance, promenade through the grounds or wander through the rooms of the big house, admiring the paintings of the famous Wentworth collection. It was the only way to see those paintings; the collection had never been on public view. Aunt Lydie said she couldn't bear to part with them that long.

The women at the party had outdone themselves to look

glamourous because a fête at The Crossing was a very special event. But none looked more glamourous than my aunt, who was dashing about in all her best diamonds and a silvery dress to match her hair. She was rosy with excitement and pleasure and altogether, in every way, splendid.

Somewhere down behind the swimming pool, fireworks were being unleashed at regular intervals, and each time a volley rocketed into the sky and sent its multicolored jewels drifting down, she exclaimed with delight. "Oh, do look!" I heard her cry as I came in. "They're like the treasures of Ali Baba! Too beautiful . . . too beautiful!"

She saw me then and hurried over to whisper in my ear like a pleased conspirator. "Do you know that all these people have brought me presents? Hannah tells me that the downstairs hall is overflowing with them. Isn't it too wonderful? I can't imagine how they found out about my birthday. I didn't breathe a word!"

I had seen the confusion downstairs; the frantic maids and even the three Wentworth chauffeurs and extra help who had been parking cars were swarming about loaded with packages. I had brought a present for her, too—a little watercolor of the Tuileries that I had done while I was in Paris. She loved the gardens, and I thought it would please her to see that I could still paint.

"I'm so glad you got back in time. I always worry about those flights being delayed. I hope you're not too tired. It probably won't catch up with you until tomorrow, if you're lucky. How was Paris and where is Gregor? "

"Paris was awful." It was worse than that. In the past, these trips had been fun. Gregor was so charming and such amusing company. But this time I had scarcely laid eyes on him. Heaven only knows where he was or what he was doing. He was absent so much that I wasn't even sure he was in the city. I suppose it all had to do with his scheme for expanding his gallery operations. "World Galleries" would be the name, with the first European branch planned for Paris. Eventually he intended to put it on the Big Board, although I knew he needed more financing before he was ready for the final steps. Whatever he was doing, he didn't confide in me, and I was left to do the regular gallery drudgery alone, feeling very sorry for myself. And there was another thing.

"He didn't come back with me. Just as we were leaving for the airport, he found that he had to go to the south of France. I came back alone." Did I sound as irritated about it as I felt? Certainly Aunt Lydie was looking at me strangely.

"Well, that's odd. I've noticed that Paris often has a strange effect on people, especially when there is a heat wave over there." Having disposed of Paris, she turned to more current things. "Now tell me who all these people are. I don't know half of them. I can't imagine how they got here. Do you suppose they came to see the pictures?"

Of course she knew them—most of them, at any rate. But it was a game she liked to play, so I played along, pointing out one or two art critics I recognized and helping her sort out and put names to some of the dozens of other people she was vaguely nodding and smiling at.

"Now who's that, for instance?" she asked, jabbing me with a diamond-studded finger.

"Why, Aunt Lydie, that's Oliver Reynolds."

"Oh, of course. The one I thought you ought to marry." (So she did know, the sly thing!) "Isn't he doing something rather interesting in your field?"

That was putting it mildly, as far as I was concerned, although I could never get used to the idea of Oliver's activities being anything but earnest and rather dull. He'd been an art critic and now he was doing films on art. "I just read that he's working on a documentary on Western art . . . Remington and Russell and Catlin and a lot of lesser-knowns."

"I see." My aunt wasn't interested in Western art. "It all sounds terribly dusty. Now who's *that*?" She wouldn't dream of pointing, so this time a little nod of her head sufficed. She meant a remarkably short and thickset man who was talking to a very tall blonde. "I know the girl; that is, I don't remember her name but she's an actress or a model, I think. I must have invited her, but the man?"

"I'm surprised you haven't read about him. He's Sidney Muss."

She turned away to say a few words to an old friend who had just finished a stint as ambassador to France, then picked up our conversation exactly where it left off. "Sidney Muss? I suppose I must have invited him or he wouldn't be here. What does he do?"

"Well, these days he's famous as an art collector—really outré contemporary stuff. Nobody is exactly sure how he made his money. I've heard everything from beer to hearses. He'd like to kill Oliver if he could."

Aunt Lydie loved it, even though she knew it was a figure of speech. "Why?"

"Because Oliver made him infamous for a while, and he's had to work like mad to wipe the egg off his reputation." I remembered it vividly. It had been a mess. "While Oliver was an art critic for the *Times,* Muss had put his whole first collection of supposed Masters on view as a charity benefit and Oliver exposed them all as fakes—every last one." It had been quite a nine-day scandal at the time. Muss had seemed to take it gracefully, stating in print that he would destroy every painting if Oliver's opinion was confirmed by other experts, which it was. But, really, it was a wonder Oliver escaped with his life. As it was, Sidney Muss was vindictive enough and had enough muscle to get Oliver fired. "The present collection is all living artists. Muss is so afraid of fakes and further humiliation that he makes most of his favorite artists work right in his house in town."

"Imagine!" She had a few words for a passing senator and his wife and then went right back to assessing Muss, taking in the clothes that were just a bit too expensive, the tan that was just a shade too tan. "I don't care for his looks," she concluded firmly.

"Well, I've heard that he has unsavory connections and that he never moves without a bodyguard."

"A bodyguard?" She was fascinated. "Do you suppose he has one here tonight?"

She looked around, hoping to see the bulge of a shoulder holster under some waiter's jacket, but none was visible. Just when I was afraid she would begin to pout, a new thought struck her. "Maybe you have some idea about it. Do you know, I notice there are people here who seem to be in costume. It's the oddest thing. Do you suppose they thought this was a costume party?"

I was thinking that one over when a voice behind me broke in. "Excuse me, Miss Wentworth. They knew it wasn't a costume party, but I can explain." It was Alida Brown. She must have been standing near us for some time, waiting to make her manners to her hostess. "Forgive me, but I couldn't help overhearing. I'm Alida Brown, and I've been so looking forward to meeting you. The costumes are for a multimedia performance Gains has arranged for you for your birthday. He's going to stage it at midnight. I hope you'll like it."

"Multimedia?" Aunt Lydie exclaimed with distaste. She could be very rude at times, particularly when she was taken by surprise, but I knew she was just striking out without thinking because this wasn't the Alida Brown she expected. Still, it sounded awful, and I cringed for Alida Brown's sake. Aunt Lydie must have had a good look at the girl at the Whitney after all.

I leapt into the breach, praying that she wouldn't say anything more. "This is Alida, Gainsborough's bride, Aunt Lydie." I spelled it out with great big pauses in between so she'd be sure to get the message.

She seemed to be having the strangest reaction—usually she was a quick study. Her expression was so blank that I had a panicky feeling she wasn't going to acknowledge the introduction at all.

"Impossible," her voice was just a murmur. "And yet I can see some likeness . . . yes, some—" Then she pulled herself together and, like a horseman executing a flying change of leads, she gathered herself together and let the

13

restrained smile expand to a gracious beam, bestowing her hand at the same time. "At last we meet. I was beginning to think it would never happen. I'm away so much of the time, you see. Now, tell me all about yourself. We'll just ignore the rest of these people and have a long talk, just the two of us. Let's just go over here and you can tell me all about the multi—what was it? I've never seen one, you know."

They drifted away together talking like old friends. And that was the last I saw of either of them for the next couple of hours. I plunged into the party and began to have fun.

You were liable to meet anyone at Aunt Lydie's. She loved to invite a mixed bag of people; it was one of the secrets of her success. In the space of a few minutes, for example, I saw two dress designers and a hairdresser, the director of the Metropolitan Museum and the general manager of the Metropolitan Opera, a tennis star and a very rich retired jockey, a superannuated debutante and a very respectable transvestite, a Yugoslav filmmaker, a Jewish novelist, a *New Yorker* cartoonist, a former mayor of New York City and the female publisher of a metropolitan newspaper, and a number of survivors of several defunct rock groups. I began to feel that only a hardened reader of both *Women's Wear Daily* and *People* magazine could fully appraise the turnout.

I also saw Gainsborough Brown in a huddle with some of the cast of his impending performance. All of them, including Gains, were enveloped in long dark cloaks. I suppose the idea was to conceal their costumes and at the same time arouse curiosity about the event to come.

Gains tore himself away to speak to me. "Hello, Persis. Where's Gregor? I thought he'd be here."

"He stayed over an extra day at the last minute."

"He told me he'd be back tonight!" He was aggressively petulant. "We have things to discuss. My contract's up soon, you know. People are interested—people who really appreciate my talent, and I'm getting offers. With all the fancy things Olitsky's planning abroad, I should think he'd need me more than ever. He'd better get on the ball."

I almost bit down hard on my tongue to keep from saying something I'd regret later. What Gains said was true—now of all times Gregor needed him in his stable to help get capital and to lend prestige to his project. On the other hand, a showcase in Paris and later in Rome, if all went well, wouldn't hurt Gains one bit. Both their pocketbooks should prosper.

"What's under those cloaks, Gainsborough? Is everyone dressed up?"

"Everyone but me. Ives is still working on mine. She's impossible lately. She takes forever to get anything done. Stupid woman, always stumbling around. She'll have to sneak it in the back way and deliver it to me as soon as she's done—which I hope to God is well before midnight." His annoyance mounted, just thinking about his late costume, and he scowled.

I asked him how he was coming along with the work for his show in the fall, and he replied that everything was almost finished, adding, with his usual modesty, that it would be the greatest display of his genius to date and that he was going to make headlines around the world. "I'll make the papers tomorrow, too. After we're done, I'm going to present Miss Wentworth with the first Gainsborough Brown sculpture. The birthday present of the century, the first Gainsborough Brown sculpture joining one of the foremost—if not *the* foremost—collections in the world!"

I had to admire him. By this one bold stroke he would finally be able to say that he was represented in the Wentworth collection. For years he'd been trying to maneuver it without success; but now, how could my aunt possibly stand there in front of all her guests and refuse his gift, no matter how much she loathed his work? Poor Aunt Lydie! She didn't know it yet, but she was cornered.

I had half an impulse to go and warn her about what she was in for, but instead I found myself out on the dance floor putting in mileage with a variety of energetic partners. It must have been around eleven when Oliver Reynolds caught up with me there and led me off to a table outside.

"It's time you took a few minutes out. You must be tired." Even in the romantic light of the flickering candle he looked stuffy as ever, though nicely stuffy. "What you need is some champagne. Stay right here while I go and track down a waiter. I'm going to blow this candle out so no one will see you while I'm gone and take you away again." I wanted to tell him that I enjoyed the dancing—what else was a party for? But he had gone loping off before I could speak, just as he'd been loping off to get things for me ever since we were children together. And maybe this time he was right. The moment I sat down I felt tired. That international malaise, jet lag, no doubt. It was a relief to lean back in my chair in the darkness, listening to the music and watching the dancers moving like skaters past the windows of the indoor court, where the orchestra was holding forth.

Groups of laughing people drifted past without seeing me, and individuals broke away, wandering off in search of other faces. Couples were close together, intoxicated by the beauty of the night and the surroundings. Everything and everyone seemed touched with mystery and magic—actors faintly seen and vaguely lighted behind a deep blue scrim.

No one appeared to notice me, and I was feeling blissfully relaxed and grateful for my enforced stint on the sidelines. Suddenly, two men's voices broke in on my privacy. They were standing in the shadows just beyond where I could distinguish shapes clearly, but through some trick of the night I could hear quite plainly what they were saying.

"If you'd rather wreck your reputation than meet my price, that's no skin off my back." The words were laced with fury.

The second spoke slowly, but each syllable struck with the impact of a bullet. "Just one thing: Play games with me and you get hurt. Understand? No question." I shrank back in my chair as far as I could. If I don't see them, they can't see me. It was a childish thought but a comforting one in proximity to such menace.

Oliver loomed up just then. Reassured by his familiar presence, I leaned forward and squinted bravely into the darkness, but the two men had disappeared.

"You're shaking like a leaf, Persis. You must be exhausted. Here, take my coat." His jacket was around my shoulders and it felt good. "I'm sorry it took me so long, but that old fool Dickie de Pauw cornered me. As usual, he was trying to seduce some young girl with tales of his derring-do back in the days when polo was in flower at the old Meadowbrook Club, and he wanted me to testify to how great he'd been. I couldn't shake him off."

The champagne was performing its usual miracle and I was feeling better immediately. "Did the girl buy it? "

"To all appearances. But then, she was a little tight, I think."

We both laughed affectionately over Dickie de Pauw, the antiquated Don Juan. Here he was, forty years after his successes behind a polo mallet, making a play for every young girl he met. It was ludicrous to see him essaying his old-fashioned, 1925-style passes. But his contemporaries were wild with envy at his sheer nerve and because his wife, Eleanore, still bothered to be jealous. It was her foremost pastime after works of charity and the restoration of historic houses like Oak Hill.

"He's such an old bore. I wonder what Eleanore sees in him?"

"She loves him, Persis, and who can explain love? It hasn't anything to do with good sense, which reminds me to say that it's good to see you again. It's been a long time since you turned me down for someone else, but you haven't changed. Now there's Olitsky, isn't there? "

Why did everyone assume that I was in love with Gregor? Had I really drawn my life into an orbit that encircled only him? "Gregor is purely business, nothing more. People get such strange ideas. Why, I can remember that they once gossiped about me and Gainsborough, of all people! "

Oliver laughed a little grimly. "I remember, too. But he's managed to get himself a nice wife somehow, hasn't he? I danced with her earlier, and she's very attractive, like a beautiful milkmaid. What do you suppose possessed her to marry an oaf like him? He has no morals and fewer scruples. Would you believe he tried to bribe me this spring? He wanted me to produce a whole series of films about him and he offered to give me some paintings from his early period if I'd do it."

I was taken aback. There weren't any paintings available that I knew of for him to give away. Besides, everything had to pass through the gallery's hands according to the contract. "What paintings?" I asked.

"I don't know. I never saw them. I told him to go to hell."

"Good." Still, I did wish he'd seen them. What could they be? Or had Gains just been talking through his hat?

"I was tempted to throw him right down the stairs, literally. And I'm sorry I didn't. Did you notice what his wife is wearing tonight?"

An odd question, coming from Oliver. He wasn't the type to fuss about women's clothes. "A white dress with a white stole, as I remember. Strange, for such a warm evening. Why?"

"Because that knitted thing is hiding bruises on her arms. The scarf slipped while we were dancing, and I couldn't help seeing. Maybe she's the type that bruises easily, I don't know. But when he passed me a few minutes ago, I wanted to knock his head off. He'd got hold of a bottle and was wandering off in the bushes to get drunk, I suppose. If we're lucky he may fall in the pool and drown."

Just at this moment Dickie de Pauw came roaring down upon us, puffing and steaming and wheezing enough for fifteen or twenty men. He was towing a tall girl behind him—a girl who was somehow familiar, a girl who was rigged up in an outerspace-type costume festooned with colored light bulbs.

"Hi, there, you two!" Dickie bellowed cheerfully. He always shouted, even when standing inches away from one. "We're off to see the fireworks up close. Suspect the best place would be somewhere near the swimming pool, wouldn't you say?" He leaned down and peered at us. Something unusual seemed to strike him. "Oh, it's you, Reynolds. Recognized Persis at once and took it for granted you were that crazy Russian. Where the hell is he, Persis? Never seen you without him."

When it came to tact, Dickie had no equal for placing the foot squarely in the mouth.

"Gregor stayed over in France on business." I was beginning to feel like a broken record.

"Russian monkey business, I'll bet. Ha, ha. Well, come on, Cinderella, let's get going if we're to see the fireworks. Have to get her back by midnight. She's in that play-acting thing." As if we couldn't guess.

The girl didn't want to move. "I have to find my cloak. Can't be in the performance without my cloak." She stood, swaying slightly, and stared at me.

"Forget the silly cloak," Dickie shouted, waving his drink around like a polo mallet.

"But Gains said it's important to have our cloaks on at the beginning so we can throw them off and surprise everyone with our costumes."

"You'll surprise them all right, honey. Hey, Oliver, do you know that these bulbs light up? She's got a battery in her belt. Show the man, honey."

"If I could just remember where I took it off when I showed you my costume ..." But Dickie was tugging at her.

"Got to go now or never. My wife will be along any minute. Got a very jealous wife, you know."

The girl was still protesting as he dragged her purposefully down the path toward the fireworks.

It couldn't have been more than two or three minutes later that the girl began screaming, horribly and regularly, with each scream ending in a rising crescendo. Oliver and I were on our feet and running instantly. I remember that I kept tripping on my long dress, and the next day I found holes where my high heels had ripped the fabric.

We met Dickie halfway up from the pool. He was toiling up the path faster than he'd moved in several decades. Poor old thing. His heart must have been pounding right out of his rib cage, and for once he couldn't even shout. "There's someone in the water . . . at the bottom of the pool. Maybe we can get him out between us. All weighted down in an overcoat or something . . . must have sunk like a rock. The girl is sure it's that artist, what's his name Brown."

"Run back to the house and see if you can get a doctor, Persis." Oliver was very cool. "And please call the police."

I don't know why I should have thought of it at a time like that. But while they were talking, I kept thinking, I know who that girl is. Of course. She's the girl at the Whitney with Gains. I knew I'd seen her before!

3

The hours that followed were interminable. They were hours I've tried to forget, but I don't suppose I ever shall. The arrival of the police ... the fruitless efforts to revive Gains, who looked strangely small with all those people working over him ... the detectives who came and asked questions. And through it all, the party kept right on going in the distance. Most of the guests didn't know what was going on down by the pool, and they must have rubbed their eyes when they read the papers the next day.

It was two o'clock before Oliver and I were able to get Alida home and to bed. There wasn't anyone else to do it. She hadn't had time to make any friends over here, and Gains was too selfish to have made real friends anywhere. She had been heartrendingly brave throughout the ordeal, never whimpering when they finally gave up on Gainsborough. The only request she made was that we call her own doctor. He was really Gains's doctor, but she wanted him. It would comfort her, she said. And when we got to the house, he was waiting with a good strong sedative and a promise to look in on her in the morning.

There weren't any servants in the house, which surprised me, and we didn't want to leave her sleeping there all alone, so we finally routed Miss Ives from her apartment above Gains's studio behind the house and asked her to stay the night with Alida and to see that she wasn't disturbed by the newspapers, which were bound to be calling any moment now.

Miss Ives behaved far worse than Alida did. We ought to have broken the news of Gainsborough's death to her gently. Certainly, I ought to have been more considerate, knowing as I did that she had waited on him hand and foot with selfless devotion, cleaning his brushes, cooking his meals, mixing his drinks, stretching his canvases and generally fulfilling the roles of both unthanked housemaid and lackey. But Oliver and I were so concerned about Alida that I'm afraid we were thoughtless; and when Miss Ives realized that Gainsborough had died, she went to pieces.

It was a long time before we got her quieted down. But finally, still blinking back tears behind her glasses, she begged us to tell her exactly what had happened, and we did our best. The police theorized that he had gone down near the swimming pool to change into his costume, where he could do so unobserved; they found his evening clothes in a pile where he had changed in the shrubbery. They also found a mostly empty bottle of champagne and a glass. They believed that he had changed into his cumbersome costume, which included boots, a heavy tunic and several lengths of chain wound around his neck and his waist; confused his direction in the dark; and instead of going back up toward the house, turned the opposite way in the dark and stepped into the black pool before realizing his mistake. Dickie de Pauw and the Whitney girl had found both of the giant, bronze, many-branched candelabras, which had been thrust into the ground to light the pool area, toppled over and burned out. Presumably they had been shaken loose by the repercussions of the fireworks. They had been top-heavy to begin with.

Dickie had picked up one of the large candles and lit it, and it was then that they saw Gains. If he had cried out while he was struggling in the water, no one would have heard above the echoing explosions of the fireworks. It was too awful. "It never would have happened if I hadn't been

22

late finishing his costume. I had all the others to do and he changed the design for his own three times. I stayed up the whole night and worked on it all day and it still wasn't finished. He told me to come in the service entrance and leave it for him down near the pool, and I did. I never even saw him. If only I had finished in time." Miss Ives was crying again.

"What was his costume supposed to represent?" Oliver was trying to distract her.

"Oh, I don't know. He kept changing his mind. And he could be, well, you know. He was very unsophisticated at times. I think everyone was going to be a nation and act the way they thought their nation would act and finally all get together in harmony and salute Miss Wentworth on her birthday. They were going to dance and sing, more or less spontaneously. He wanted to have electronic sound effects. Everything today is electronic, he said. But there wasn't time. It would have been much more effective."

"And his costume?"

"Why, Russia, of course. All those peasants enchained by their government and the Russian ideology."

"Good God," exclaimed Oliver.

We left after that, staggering with fatigue. Miss Ives was still sitting there nodding her head, two rivulets of tears sliding beneath her glasses and dropping unheeded on the front of her shapeless cotton wrapper.

Poor Miss Ives, I thought. She was probably in love with that big brute. I never suspected it, but I'll bet she was. Poor, poor mousy thing. She would have to fall for the one man who would never make passes at a girl who wore glasses because he was so hung up on the beauty of women's eyes!

4

None of us knew where to get in touch with Gregor, so we just had to wait. But not for long. He appeared the next afternoon and took charge of matters with a vigor that bordered on downright enthusiasm, channeling all of his considerable talents into making Gainsborough's death—which had occurred, after all, under rather bizarre circumstances—a logical and thoroughly memorable tragedy. Artists, he made clear, weren't expected to be athletes or know how to do practical things like swimming. Artists could be expected to deck themselves out in chains and fall into pools. Artists were different. They even died in unconventional ways.

If he was personally upset by the loss of his most lucrative painter, he concealed it well. Oh, he displayed grief, all right, but it didn't ring true. It was too professional, like the way a politician pays tribute to a fallen rival.

Alida fought to keep him from turning Gains's funeral into a public spectacle, and consequently he fumed with frustration throughout the quiet private services. Afterward he held press conferences day after day, releasing tidbits of information with such skill that the Gainsborough Brown story was more alive than when the hero himself had been on the scene to contribute to the legend.

"We have just learned from his widow that the artist was suffering from severe exhaustion the last weeks of his life. He refused to see his doctor despite his wife's pleas, saying he could not spare the time from preparation of the oeuvres for an exhibition slated for September, but now postponed indefinitely."

"Word has just reached us from Paris of the sale of a hitherto unknown Gainsborough Brown sold recently for $79,000 to an anonymous collector. During his last sojourn in France, Brown left the picture with a Paris dealer with instructions that proceeds from the sale go to support a penniless French painter he knew. As was his custom in all his good deeds, Brown stipulated that no names were to be revealed."

"Six prominent collectors today established a Gainsborough Brown Purchase Award, the recipient to be selected from a national competition."

I guess some of it was true; but with Gregor and his flair for publicity, one could never be certain. For instance, I suspected that the "exhaustion" Alida spoke of was brought on more by a bout of drinking than by overwork, and she was too naive to know it. And since when would Gains give away $79,000 to a penniless French painter, or anyone else? However, the story about the purchase award was doubtless authentic, as well as a certain percentage of the others Gregor released throughout July and August as he kept the Gainsborough Brown pot boiling.

Naturally, all of this couldn't happen without Gregor himself attracting a share of the attention. In the space of a few weeks, he became a celebrity of sorts. People who wouldn't dream of buying a picture themselves knew that he had been Gainsborough's dealer, that he maintained a New York office and that he owned a string of galleries, with plans to open several others in Europe. He was flooded with requests to serve on art juries, to write articles for magazines, to speak at colleges and universities. He even began to be recognized on the street, the surest proof of a big press.

Another move Gregor made was to order the closing of

all his galleries for a period of two months. The front door of the local one, the North Shore gallery, was locked. Anyone who peered through the huge plate-glass window saw nothing inside—the big room was empty. Overnight he had had the walls of the main gallery and the outside front façade of the building painted black. The same was done to all the others in the chain. We were in stark, dramatic mourning for Gainsborough Brown.

But back in the office there was frantic activity. The telephones never stopped ringing. Mountains of mail about Gains piled up. The extra help we had to hire scurried about getting in everyone's way. The regular staff was so overworked they all threatened to quit. I was trying to rearrange the schedules for all the galleries, with the attending headaches, and still cope with everything that was going on around me. All the problems seemed to land on my desk, Gregor having made himself unavailable.

Not that he wasn't working. Clouds of smoke billowed out from underneath the door of the plush suite where he and his secretary, Mrs. Withers, closeted themselves all day with four telephones and a constantly replenished supply of Scotch. The Scotch was for Mrs. W., a rugged old veteran of the secretarial wars who looked like a survivor of the disagreement between the Medes and the Persians. The smoke was hers, too. She lived on a combination of drink and cigarettes, and the mixture worked within her chemically to maintain a constant state of mental efficiency and physical near-paralysis. After a trip to the closet where her favorite elixir was kept, she could add columns of six-figure numbers in her head. She could remember the dimensions of a picture sold ten years ago. She could recall the name, age and school grade of a client's child. So Gregor considered her awesome breath a small price to pay for such virtues.

The two of them, locked in their private little inferno, forgot about me for days on end, and I was too busy to worry about it. Occasionally I heard them on the telephone as I passed their door, and once I heard Gregor shouting to someone who must have been in France, "I have the papers here, comprenez vous? Ici! Pourquoi vous n'avez pas sent it? Envoyez? It's not in Customs here. La Douane. Comprenez? Pas ici!" I tapped on the door and asked Gregor if I could help him—anything in French was usually my job. So were pictures in Customs. But he roared at me so ferociously that I hurried away, puzzled and hurt. What was the big secret?

It had always been traditional for us to have dinner together on nights when we worked late, and we still did. But now he never failed to have Mrs. Withers in tow. Was he afraid to be alone with me, all of a sudden? Were there questions he didn't want me to ask and so he brought along a third person as insurance? He said he feared Mrs. W. would fall apart if he didn't feed her after a hard day's work, but he had never exhibited such solicitousness before.

It was on one of those nights when the three of us were having a quick late dinner that he said, "I want you to go see Alida Brown."

"I'd love to. In fact I've tried to a dozen times," I replied. "But ever since that first night and a quick glimpse of her at the funeral she's shut me out. Each time I call, her maid says that she's not seeing anyone."

"I know. I've had the same experience. But she'll see you now because there's a problem. You know how Gains always kept his studio locked?" Indeed I did know. It was an old joke among people who knew Gains. Every day he went to his studio in the late morning and locked himself in. We used to say that he really went there to sleep or to drink because he produced so little work that we couldn't think of any other explanation. The door was also locked when he wasn't in his studio, and he never allowed anyone except Miss Ives to have the key because, we were sure, he didn't want anyone to find out how little he accomplished during the day.

"The problem is," Gregor continued, "that the studio is *still* locked."

"You mean you haven't been down there? You haven't

seen the new work?" I was aghast. "Doesn't his wife have a key?"

"No, I haven't and no, she doesn't. It's absurd. It seems she's never had a key. I hated to bother her, but the other day I finally asked to see what Gains had done for this fall. And she said she'd never even seen the inside of his studio."

"Incredible! Then why doesn't she have the door taken off or something?"

"Not necessary," said Gregor. "Miss Ives has a key. And, according to Alida, Miss Ives says that Gains told her if anything ever happened to him, you were the only person she was to let open the studio door. Alida insists it's true. The door is not to be opened unless you, Persis, are present. Miss Ives apparently said she'd call the police if Alida went near that studio. Wouldn't that make one hell of a rumpus! You can imagine that Alida is a little put out, so what I want you to do is go over and smooth her feathers and then get the key from Ives."

"But that's insane," I exclaimed. "Why would Gains do a thing like that? It makes me feel like a fool. What must Alida think? Why would he have done that?"

Gregor and Mrs. W., who hadn't opened her mouth, sat and looked at me. At least, I think Mrs. W. was looking at me. Sometimes it was hard to tell with her. And for the first time since I'd known him there was a definite unfriendliness in Gregor's expression.

"I thought you'd know the answer to that," he said.

But I certainly didn't.

5

It was after I went to see Alida Brown that I began to keep
the sketchbook that was to come very close to costing me
my life. I don't know why I began it exactly. Something
about the visit was unsettling—something I couldn't quite
put my finger on. So I began to make quick sketches of
anything I saw or remembered that had to do with the
subject of Gains, using any scrap of paper at hand if I
didn't happen to be carrying my sketchbook. It was a form
of automatic writing, completely spontaneous, my own
way of clarifying my thoughts. Surprising how often things
appeared on my drawing pad that I didn't even know
were in my head! I called it my Gainsborough Brown
book, and I didn't mention it to anyone for the simple
reason that I wouldn't have known how to explain it.

It was with a certain amount of trepidation that I went
to call on Alida. The episode of the key mortified me; I
couldn't think how to handle it gracefully. But at the same
time I was anxious to see her and to help her in any way I
could. The poor creature was so alone. To my knowledge
no member of either her family or Gains's family (if he had
one) had been at her side to help her through the funeral
and the difficult time afterward. And here she was in a
strange country—a widow almost before she had had time
to be a bride.

I wheeled my little Mustang down the winding driveway, watching the house come into view and wondering what had possessed Gains to install his new wife in such a dilapidated place. Not that the old house wasn't beautiful—it was. In Long Island's heyday fifty years ago, its arching porches and airy drawing rooms had been filled with guests. The stables where Gains had made a studio had housed the best in horseflesh, polo ponies and hunters in roomy box stalls, the hardware and nameplates flashing with hand-burnished brass. And in the back halls and kitchens of the old house a company of servants had scurried around—the indispensable props of gracious living. How many empty bedrooms on the third floor had contained these workers? How many gardeners had it taken to manicure these now forsaken grounds? How many grooms to manicure the horses?

There was still beauty, and there were signs that Gains had made a start at fixing the place up. The front was freshly painted and there were sections of new fence around the service entrance. I remembered the rumors that Alida came from a rich family. That must be it, I thought. He was planning a new life as a country gentleman with a big house, a wealthy wife and everything that went with it. Onward and up the social scale with Gainsborough Brown.

It was a minute or two before there was any response to my knock; then I heard the unmistakable sound of bolts being drawn on the other side of the heavy front door, and it finally swung open. A cheerful little maid welcomed me into the wide hallway I remembered from the night Oliver and I had brought Alida home. The mural wallpaper that lined the walls was as faded and dreary by daylight as it had been in the dark, and the fine English paneling had been so neglected that it cried out for attention.

Mrs. Brown, I was told, was not feeling well. Would I mind going upstairs to her bedroom to see her? I waited while the maid locked the front door again and then followed her up the curving stairway to a bedroom at the far end of an upstairs hall lined with closed doors.

Alida's bedroom was as shabby as every other room I'd

seen here, and her fourposter bed must have come with the house because it was built in. But there was nothing shabby about the meringue of white pillows that were propped behind her head or the delicate sheets and batiste coverlet, all lavishly monogrammed with a flourish of initials I couldn't read. In spite of its being a humid day with the thermometer hovering in the high eighties, the windows in her room were closed and the blinds drawn, making the atmosphere in the room so stifling that I could hardly breathe.

"Oh, Alida, wouldn't you like me to open the windows? There's a breeze just beginning to stir."

"No, please! The windows are locked. They must stay that way. There's a balcony outside, and it would be easy for someone to break in here, wouldn't it, Maggie?"

"Yes, ma'am, I guess it would." The maid, Maggie, turned to me and explained, "There are outside stairs at each side of the door at this end of the downstairs hall that go up to the two outside balconies. It's very pretty. If you'll excuse me now, I'll go and bring the tea." She smiled at us and went out.

I thought of the front door bolted in broad daylight and knew it wasn't a joke. "But why would anyone want to break into your house, Alida?"

"I don't know. Believe me, there's nothing here. No money. And all of Gainsborough's work is in the studio." Although she wasn't a small girl, she looked as pale and unprotected as a child, lying in that big bed that could have held four of her with ease—the kind of girl who is brought up since infancy with a Nanny to hold a parasol over her head in the sun and an umbrella in the rain. She looked like a girl who had always been protected. And now she was alone—and frightened.

"Something did happen the night Gainsborough died, Persis. Someone was looking for something here. The next day all sorts of little things were out of place, as if someone had been searching for something. One knows when things are out of place in one's own house. As I said, little things—

31

a vase ... magazines ... drawers not quite closed ... you know what I mean." The light, scarcely accented voice was almost a whisper.

"I can understand how you feel," I told her soothingly. "And I want you to know how embarrassed I am about this business of the studio. I can't understand it. All I can say is that I'm sorry. And I wonder, could it have been Miss Ives looking for the studio keys?"

"Oh, no. Lately Gains never carried them. He said he'd lost them too many times. They were always left with her."

I believed it. Gainsborough was too lazy to do anything he didn't want to bother to do, including remember where he'd put his own keys.

"But it must have been Miss Ives, Persis." She was frowning. "No one else was here that night except you and Oliver and the doctor. The servants had all left several days before. So there must be something in this house she wants. I'm afraid of her."

Poor Alida! Afraid of Miss Ives!

"You need someone here to look after you. Has the doctor been in to see you?"

"Oh, yes. He comes almost every day. He's so kind. I'm not really sick, I know. He says it's shock, quite natural under the circumstances was the way he put it. He's given me all these pills."

"I'm glad to hear that he's looking after you. But what about the rest of the time? You ought to let people come and see you. I've tried so many times. And what about your family?"

"No, no. I don't need anyone." She was too emphatic, I thought, too close to the edge. "The doctor says I'll be better soon. But he doesn't want me to have any excitement. And Maggie's here. She's very good to me; she knows just how I like things. She stays here at night, now. You see, I haven't lived here long enough to have friends I can trust." Her voice broke a little. "I hardly even knew Gainsborough, we were married such a short time." Her hands began to shake and she clasped them tightly together until she had them under control.

"Please tell me what I can do. I'd like to help. And don't ever think you haven't any friends. I want to be your friend and so do more people than you can imagine. Just give us a chance, Alida."

"Thank you. You're very kind. I'll remember." There was a tap on the bedroom door. "That will be Maggie with the tea. Come in!"

Maggie had fixed a beautiful tray of iced tea and thin sandwiches, which she placed next to me while she fussed over Alida, plumping out her pillows and laying out two pills from the array of bottles on her bedside table. As she left, Alida asked her to be sure to close the door, and she did.

"I don't want her to walk in and interrupt," she explained, as I gave her her tea. "I'm really glad you came today because I have something for you which may or may not be important, I don't know. I decided you were the one person I could trust because my husband trusted you. He said you were the one honest person he knew. That's why he wanted you to be present when the studio was opened. I've been thinking about it for a long time, and now I've decided it's the right thing to do." She started to get out of bed and then sank back again. "Would you mind, Persis? I feel a little dizzy. It must be those pills. I'm so sorry."

"Of course, I don't mind." I jumped up. "What can I do?" They had to be fast-acting pills. I hadn't even seen her take them.

"There's something I want you to keep for me. I can't send it to the gallery for safekeeping because then Gregor would have access to it and I'm not sure how he felt about my husband. There was some trouble between them, I know. Gainsborough was looking for a New York gallery. He said they'd reached the point where he was more valuable to Gregor Olitsky than Gregor was to him—so it has to be you." Alida pointed toward her dressing room. "Look in my closet. There's a pink and white hatbox on the top shelf. You will find another box inside it—an old, brown, wooden box with a lid. I found it in Gainsborough's room when Maggie and I were cleaning it out. I had never seen it before; he must have kept it out of sight. Nothing inside makes any particular sense to me, but it might to you. After all, you've known Gainsborough longer than I have. Please take it and keep it. It's the only thing here I can think of that might have any possible value."

I followed her directions and found the box. Her closet was a triumph of good order: dresses, shoes and a row of hatboxes. I could see why she would notice if a single magazine had been moved an inch. The box was neatly tied with a white string.

"I'll look after it, Alida," I promised. "And I'll even look into it if that's what you want, and let you know if anything there is important. But I'll feel as if I were prying."

She sighed. "You remind me of my father. He always said that prying was a worse sin than lying and that his privacy was his most treasured possession. We weren't very close. He is a very private person. My mother died when I was born. You asked about my family. Well, my father didn't want me to marry Gainsborough. I wrote him before Gains . . . before it happened, but he never answered. My father is old-fashioned." She turned her face to the wall so that I wouldn't see her cry.

I should write him, I thought. His daughter is in trouble and he ought to know about it, old-fashioned or not.

Then I remembered why I was here. "Do you want me to get the studio key from Miss Ives? Where is she? I'll get it for you now."

Alida had composed herself. "I suppose she's in her apartment over the studio; she lives there, you know. Persis, I'm so afraid of her. I know she hates me. She looks at me as if she wants me dead. You can't imagine how frightened I was when I found myself in the house with her after Gainsborough died."

"But she didn't hurt you, did she?" I wanted to calm her. And by no stretch of imagination could I picture colorless

Miss Ives as a menace. "Don't worry so much. Nobody hates you and nobody's going to hurt you. You're getting better; and once you're on your feet and feeling well again, you'll realize that everyone, including Miss Ives, is your friend."

Alida was drowsy now. Her eyes were almost closed. "Keys," she murmured, "keys."

"I'm going to get them now."

She roused herself briefly. "Do as my husband said. You open the studio yourself. And please lock my bedroom door when you go out and give the key to Maggie. I have another one in my table drawer. It's important to keep doors locked. I must be safe."

Her eyes were shut and she was breathing regularly when I went out, locking the door behind me. I was so upset by Alida's physical and emotional condition and so exhausted by the heat in that airless and stifling bedroom that I actually felt faint.

Maggie was waiting when I finally reached the downstairs hall. She, too, looked worried. "Did Mrs. Brown eat anything, ma'am?"

"No, she didn't, Maggie. And she didn't touch her iced tea either. What does the doctor say?"

"He says that she'll be all right. It's mostly emotional. He says time will cure it. But it's been so long, Mrs. Willum."

"I know." I handed Maggie the bedroom key. "Does Mrs. Brown keep everything locked up like this all the time?"

"Oh, yes, ma'am." It came in a rush. "All the windows. The door to her room. Everything bolted during the day. And she doesn't sleep nights—only a little bit in the daytime. At first I slept in the next bedroom to be near her at night, but I had to move. All night long with the radio or the television going. And the light on. Like she was afraid to shut her eyes. And then I couldn't sleep for the noise and for worrying about her. She's scared for me to leave the house. I haven't had a day off since I came."

"Isn't there any other help?"

35

She shook her head.

"Wasn't there a chauffeur?" I was sure I remembered something about Alida's having brought one with her from France. It had seemed such a chic touch.

"I never heard of a chauffeur. And there wasn't any help at all when I came. I heard they left because they didn't get paid, but I'm not one to gossip. I have to do this whole house myself, plus the cooking and marketing. I don't mind because I'm sorry for that poor little thing upstairs, but it's a lot of work."

I could imagine. "That's a shame, Maggie. It's too much for one person. Couldn't you at least find someone to fill in for you for a few days so you could get a rest?"

"I tried that, ma'am. I told her my sister would come instead of me, but she got so upset I gave it up."

The more I heard about Alida, the more concerned I became. "I'll tell you what, Maggie. You see if she'll be willing to let me look after her for a day or so. I'm a pretty fair cook, and I promise I'll take good care of her for you. If she agrees, let me know. I'll be glad to do it. I'm very fond of Mrs. Brown."

Maggie was so pleased that I felt cheerful for the first time since I'd been there. As the bolts slid shut on the door behind me, I drew a deep breath of the stagnant afternoon air, and it felt like the breath of spring after the atmosphere of the place I had just left.

It was so late by now and I was so wilted that I decided I couldn't survive another emotional interview and (remembering her tears) I was sure Miss Ives would be emotional. She would have to wait until tomorrow. And when I got home I was glad I hadn't trudged the extra steps to her apartment because there was a note from her in my mail. It was the first note I'd ever had from her. Our other communication had always been business, composed largely of numbers and cryptic abbreviations and initials—the usual interoffice hieroglyphics. This was a note—a real one—in beautiful, precise handwriting that was very different from her scribbled, slap-dash, everyday communication.

Dear Mrs. Willum,

I'm sending you this key to Mr. Brown's studio because I didn't want to be responsible for it since I'm going away for a few days. The gallery was closed, so here it is. Gainsborough Brown always trusted you more than anybody, so I'm glad you will be present when his studio is opened up. If I can be of assistance in cataloguing the new work, I will be happy to do so. I will return late Friday.

Sincerely,
Hope Ives

There was something very warm and personal about her having written me a note. It made me think of her momentarily as a woman instead of a mouse. I read it over again once more before I put it away in my desk and dropped the key into my purse.

6

That night I finally did what, without realizing it, I had been putting off doing for weeks: I really seriously thought about the entire matter of Gainsborough Brown's death.

Mrs. Howard, my "houseworker" (the title was of her own choosing and she insisted on its being used), had left a hot dinner for me in the oven as was her custom before she left for the day. Her dinners weren't exactly a gourmet's delight—her talents ran more to nonstop conversation and Irish good humor—but I took the tray into the library and ploughed into the offering without being aware of what I was eating, too involved in my thoughts to notice. Later I poured some coffee and sat down with the box Alida had given me.

One by one I took out the contents and spread them on the table in front of me, examining each with equal care, taking my time. If Alida was correct and someone had searched her house for this box, something among the contents must have made it worth the trouble.

I puzzled over it for a good hour, and in the end I reached two conclusions: One, that if he had gone a step further, Gains would have been the kind of man who saved old bottle caps; and two, that he had compiled a veritable dossier on Lydie Wentworth and had made the beginnings of another on Sidney Muss, the collector. Heaven knows for what reason.

The bottle-cap side of his personality showed up in a grubby array of carefully hoarded stubs and receipts for such everyday things as dry cleaning and registered mail. There was an assortment of foreign coins in small change, which he must have forgotten to reconvert. A few old telephone bills, very large. European hotel bills, also very large. The remains of a billfold he seemingly couldn't part with. None of it was very illuminating.

The rest of the material, on the other hand, gave me something to think about. There were dozens of clippings about my aunt from newspapers and magazines, foreign and domestic. Many were photostated. They dated back, in some cases, as much as thirty years. All of them had two elements in common: They showed photographs of Aunt Lydie all over the world (she was good copy everywhere), and there was always a man—always different, rarely clearly visible, seldom identified, present in only the most casual way, but always there. I recognized none of them. They could have been current celebrities or minor local functionaries for all I could tell.

The Muss clippings made a smaller pile but were just as fascinating. They had been written for a variety of reasons—the scandal when his collection turned out to be fake, the gift he made to the Martin Luther King fund, his fantastic New York apartment, the studio where he made his artists paint, the party he gave where everyone wore handpainted clothes—things like that. In other words, his history from the time he first burst into print.

Then there were three other things. There was a color photograph from *Match* of a younger Alida waiting in line to get in to see Gainsborough's first exposure in Paris. He was one of thirteen artists (you could barely see their names on the large poster background) in the exhibition of Young Americans that had been arranged by one of our museums. It had been a smashing success. Alida must have saved the picture and given it to Gains when they met. She was standing with an older woman who was turned three quarters away from the camera.

There was an ancient debutante picture of me with tightly waved hair, which noted that I was Lydia Wentworth's niece. And there was a curling snapshot, creased and dirty, of a pleasant young girl smiling tentatively out from beneath a summer straw hat. An old love? His first wife?

I looked through it all. I studied every picture. I lingered over every word. There was something Gains had considered to be of value buried here, but what was it? In the end I put everything carefully back in the box, replaced the cover, retied the white string and put it away under the window seat in the library.

Next I went to my desk, where I had stored the newspaper accounts of Gains's death, and read them over again. What was I looking for? I didn't know. Maybe I just wanted to refresh my memory. Anyway, there was nothing new. The body had been discovered by Richard de Pauw ("former polo great") and twenty-two-year-old Susan Evans, an actress scheduled to participate in a multimedia event planned for midnight. I had tried days before to locate Susan Evans, a vague disquiet urging me on in the search. I had tried to track her down through AFTRA, the Screen Actors' Guild, the Players' Guide and the theatrical answering services. None listed her. I had even made contact with the rest of the troupe Gains had assembled at Aunt Lydie's that night, but none of them admitted to knowing anything about her.

One of the papers had picked up the bit about Gains's giving my aunt his first work of sculpture as a birthday present; but the work was already safely out of sight so it couldn't be photographed, and she herself wasn't around to comment on how she liked it. There was more, of course, but nothing with which I wasn't already familiar.

On impulse I got out the Nassau telephone book and took a crack at finding Mrs. Withers. I'd never called her at home before, and I only half expected to have any luck, but there she was under Withers, George H.

She answered on the third ring, sounding as if she had a

mouthful of glue. Good, I thought. She's already halfway to oblivion. With any luck I can get some answers before she realizes Gregor isn't with me. And tomorrow she'll probably have forgotten that I called.

"I'm sorry to call you at home, but we're having an emergency." I did my best to make my voice urgent.

"Glod to holp." Her teeth must have been tangled up in her tongue.

"We're absolutely banking on your fabulous memory, Mrs. Withers. We're going to be lost if you can't remember. I realize that it's expecting a great deal, even from you."

She snorted. I could imagine her very beads rattling with indignation. "Shirt-ly com 'member!"

"Well, then, exactly how many pictures did Mr. Olitsky get in France and where and so on?" All that mysterious talk to Paris about Customs and papers from Gregor's office had to have something to do with pictures.

There was a pause at the other end. I sat with my pencil poised, not even breathing. Would she tell me? Would she remember in her present state?

She remembered, all right, and my appeal to her pride must have fired up all her corpuscles because she began to hurl data at me with the impersonal accuracy of a computer.

"Mr. Olitsky ought to recall this himself. I don't know how he remembers to go to bed without me to remind him. He purchased three Gainsborough Browns on his last trip to Paris from three different sources. One has yet to arrive—minor difficulties. Here are the facts about the other two—the approximate date the pictures were painted, the date the artist sold them, the name of the buyer and the exact purchase price by us. I hope you have a pencil." She began to give me the information at breakneck speed while I wrote furiously, trying to keep up. Her teeth had come unstuck from the glue. She didn't slur a word. It was a remarkable performance, considering her condition. Finally she stopped.

"You're a miracle, Mrs. Withers." I meant it. "We're so

grateful. I wonder if you could possibly help with a couple of other details?"

"Name them," she snapped, very much on her mettle.

"Could you give us the name and address of Mrs. Brown's father?" Someone ought to write him and tell him the state Alida was in.

She was out of patience. "Really, Mrs. Willum, if you and Mr. Olitsky paid any attention to your clipping service, you'd know. Baron du Prey, Paris."

"Don't bother to follow up on it. It isn't necessary. That's sufficient." I tried one more thing. Miss Ives had gone off for a few days. Did Mrs. Withers have any idea where she went when she left town?

But my luck had run out. The fantastic human memory machine gave it all up. "Mr. Withers is very angry. He says I've been on the telephone too long. Good night, Mrs. Willum." And she hung up, just like that.

I needed a drink myself by now, so I poured a small brandy and studied the notes I'd taken of the conversation. Three early Gainsborough Browns from what many collectors considered his most desirable period, much as many of them preferred Picasso's "blue" period. Three pictures I had never heard of. Two of them sold in Paris by Gainsborough about the time he was courting Alida and bought back by Gregor on our stay there. Obviously sold by Gains at a fraction of the going price for a signed Gainsborough Brown of the period or Gregor could never have bought them back so cheaply, and probably sold to finance an expensive courtship of Alida. But why peddle them abroad? Why not go through his dealer, as always? Why part with them for a pittance of their true value? And where had they come from in the first place? Were they the same pictures offered to Oliver? We had no record of any unsold pictures from the early stage of his career. Every catalogued early Gainsborough Brown had long since gone into either a museum or an important collection.

It was very puzzling, but the thing that puzzled me most was that Gregor hadn't told me about it. This was a gallery matter; and as Gainsborough's original sponsor, all matters pertaining to his career were my responsibility. So why wouldn't Gregor tell me? Was this the reason for his strange behavior in France, and for his stay over?

Even though I felt a bit of a fool doing it, I lit a match and touched it to the notes I had just taken. If Gregor cared enough to keep this information a secret, I would oblige by doing the same. When the paper was reduced to ashes and thrown in the scrap basket, I pulled out my sketchbook and began to draw, feeling for the lines at first and then working more and more surely. As the pencil flashed across the page, the familiar exercise released my imagination and I began to talk to myself as I worked, trying out the fit of the words and listening to them as to the arguments of a second person.

"I don't believe Gains had too much to drink the night of the party. They assume that's why he fell in the pool, but they didn't know his capacity. Too much for anyone else was like lemonade for him." I began a sketch of Gains and his troupe of performers as I had seen them at the party, huddled together in their cloaks. He had surely been more or less sober then. "To begin with, he was a solitary drinker. His binges took place behind the locked door of his studio. And that night, of all nights, he would be moderately sober. He'd never bungle his chance to show off in front of all those social types. So he was not drunk."

I flipped the page and began to draw Gains and Susan Evans as I had seen them together outside the Whitney. "He knew perfectly well the pool was there—or he should have. I had taken him there once when I had a swim. He had wanted to come with me, hoping Aunt Lydie would be there and that he could persuade her to buy one of his pictures. He couldn't stand it because she didn't like his work."

I scratched away at the drawing some more, adding savage black marks for rain and almost obliterating Susan's face in the process, the face that ought to have been Alida's. "If he went down so close to the pool, it must have been for a reason ... to change his costume is probably right since Miss Ives was bringing it late. Could the extra glass have been for her? No, he would never be that thoughtful."

I started a new sheet, struggling for the essence of Miss Ives. "Mousy. Those eternal glasses. Nondescript hair. Doesn't say much. Doesn't drive. Keeps in background. Like a wraith, hovering around. No, that's not it. Like a mother hen, except silent. No, too frail for a mother hen. That's it—frail, bent over like a person in hiding or in pain. Probably both, working for him!" I was beginning to get her now. "Let's see. He had a bottle and a glass—the bottle for him (he never bothered with the niceties of drinking) and the glass ... for whom? His wife? Someone else's wife? Susan Evans? A man? Certainly any of those people in cloaks could have walked off with him without being identified. And what about the torchères—couldn't they have been knocked over, afterward, by a human hand? To make it look like an accident?"

I stared at the sketch of Miss Ives, wondering what I was trying to tell myself and at the same time knowing. As I stared, wearily, my imagination played one of those disconcerting tricks imagination often plays on a painter; and line by line, as surely as if guided by the pencil I was holding, a new face superimposed itself on the one I had just finished. There were the familiar, humorous eyes. The jaunty little moustache. There was the vigorous body, so ready for anything. There, more real than I could have done at my best, was Gregor.

"No!" I cried. Everything Gregor had done was perfectly normal. If the dealers' grapevine told him there were Gainsborough Browns being sold abroad—as no doubt it had—of course he'd buy them up. As for being strange with me, he might even think I was involved. It was inconceivable, but he might. And anyway, he hadn't even been present the night Gains died. No!

I seized the pencil more firmly and began a fresh page, working swiftly. A new picture took shape with lightning strokes. When it was finished, I closed the book and pushed it back as far as I could in my desk drawer. I didn't want to look at it—it was too frightening. I didn't need to look. The drawing was all too clear in my mind. Two figures locked in struggle at the edge of a dark pool, candles casting uneven light and shadow over them, and one of the figures falling backward . . . backward . . . into the black water.

It was a picture of a murder being committed.

7

"Well," said Gregor, "I must say I'm nervous. I always have been at this point, every single time—haven't you? But I guess this particular occasion will never be repeated. I find it difficult to believe."

He was dressed for "this particular occasion" in pale-pink corduroy slacks, a blue Cardin blazer embellished with the horsehead-relief buttons of the French Jockey Club, a pink shirt and a silk foulard exquisitely tied and folded. We were standing in front of Gains's studio, which was situated about two hundred yards from Alida's house and surrounded by a collection of still-standing paddocks. He and I were vacillating, putting off the moment when we would put the key in the lock and open the door to the room where Gains had done his last work.

I knew what Gregor meant about being nervous. Gainsborough's studios have always been sacrosanct. Once each year he invited us to view his accomplishments of the previous twelve months, presiding over the visits with an attitude of awe at the magnitude of his own talents and expecting the same of us. Otherwise we weren't welcome. Now and again he would bring a picture to the gallery for us to see, but we simply did not go to his studio without his special invitation. It was unthinkable.

Only one person had come and gone as she pleased and that was Miss Ives. No matter where Gains happened to be working, she always had complete run of the place. But that was to be expected—he needed her around to wait on him. Here he had installed her in the apartment directly overhead so that she would be readily available at his beck and call.

"I keep expecting him to come to the door and tell us we can't come in," I said, under my breath.

We stood on the cobblestoned court and stared at the cross-barred and timbered door in front of us, remembering past visits to other of his workrooms, recalling the uneasy anticipation with which we had waited for the unveiling of each new year's work, hearing again the offensive voice, with its scarcely concealed snarl, offering its invariable and deliberately insulting words of greeting: "OK, you merchants, come in and get your slice of my talent." How we hated him at that moment! How I longed to tell him that without the aid of other people's talent— Gregor's, in particular—he wouldn't be where he was today! But I never said it. What would be the use?

In the beginning Gainsborough's work had attained a minor success because it was so different. His rather feminine treatment of nature in his canvases was painstakingly exact. No petal was too small, no pebble too unimportant to his loving eye; and if you formed a small circle with your fingers and placed it at random over any part of the landscape of one of these paintings, that part revealed itself to be a beautiful and microscopically perfect vignette in itself.

But then there was the paradox. He insisted on putting people in these idyllic scenes and his people, while not quite stick figures, were primitive and gauche, tight and stiff, as if painted with indifference or by a hand that had no talent for the human figure. In any event, the total effect was intriguing; and when his style changed, as it did later, these early pictures became very desirable.

"Look at those trees," we would hear a collector say. "He certainly catches the feeling of the landscape. Before I owned this picture, I never paid any attention to trees.

Now I find myself looking at them all the time, and they're beautiful. But look at the way he does those people. He's telling us something. Like nature is beautiful and people are ugly. Like nature is good and people are bad. And it's true, isn't it? People are ruining nature. Look at us Americans ruining America. Why, this picture makes me feel almost religious."

It was all nonsense. As far as we could see, Gainsborough wasn't trying to say anything in his work. It was just the way he painted. The truth was that he'd never showed any signs in everyday life of liking either people or nature. He was too busy liking Gainsborough Brown.

In time his work changed. I wouldn't say it got better, but it became more cohesive, more of a piece, simpler in form. Intellectual, if that's the right word. He was smart enough to listen to his clients and to incorporate the elements of paradox on a larger scale, and he did it from then on. He painted a huge leg in a heavy boot trampling down a delicate blossom. He titled it *It Is Better to Die in Full Flower*. It immediately became a famous picture. It didn't tax the imagination too much, and it was easy to remember the title and discuss it at cocktail parties. He did a family of surburban grotesques settling down to defile a wooded glade with cans of soda and a junk food picnic, calling it *This Was Why He Made the World?* He did a hairy workman hammering up a builder's sign in front of a lovely meadow and called it *I Look and See Nothing Worth Seeing*. He even became famous for his titles. A museum bought that one.

In short, he turned himself into almost the only artist in America that the public really "dug." Anyone could understand his pictures—the message was loud and clear, like a television commercial. No one dared to quarrel with that message. It would be like criticizing Mom's apple dumplings. Even the critics fell in line. Poor things, you couldn't blame them. They'd been bombarded for years on all sides by work they were hard-pressed to understand, let alone describe at any length without resorting to a jargon that made little sense to their readers.

The trouble was that it took Gains forever to paint anything. We were never sure whether it was because of his natural sloth, his painstaking technique or his preference for parties, drinking and hanging around on the fringes of whatever segment of the jet set would accommodate him. Before long he began to complain about the amount of work he had to do and about the size of Gregor's commission, although it was the standard percentage. He grew more devoted to his pleasures than to his easel, and his pleasures cost a great deal of money.

His last show had been a crisis, and only Gregor's genius as an entrepreneur had saved it from total disaster. As the time for the exhibition approached, everyone except Gains was in a state of panic because he admitted that he hadn't completed a single picture he considered worthy. He wasn't apologetic; he was savage.

"Look," he snarled, "there are fifteen guys in this country who throw a bunch of junk together and get prices as high as I do. They get *more* publicity! So why should I kill myself? To fill *your* pockets? I'm the one who does all the work, after all. All you do is sit back and take the money. You want a show? I'll tell you what I'll do. I'll have a hundred rolls of toilet paper cast in bronze and that will be my show." He locked himself in his studio with a case of whiskey and that seemed to be that. Even Gregor's offer to cut the size of his commission—a move he made in desperation—had no effect.

But Gregor wasn't through yet. He stayed up night and day, pulling every string he knew, until he persuaded the directors of two important foreign museums to fly in for the preview. When Gains heard the news, he turned out an entire show within two weeks.

But what a show! When we first saw it all together, every hair of Gregor's luxuriously thatched head stood on end. His usually debonair expression melted like a pudding in a bag, and I know that I turned pale.

"Why, that bastard," Gregor whispered. "We're going to

be tarred and feathered!" And I wouldn't have given you any odds at all on his being wrong. Every single picture looked as if it had been put together by a blind man with the aid of a dirty floor mop, a paste pot and free access to all the empty lots in town. I wanted to go somewhere and be sick. Here we were with the invitations already out and thousands of dollars spent in advertising, with critics, clients and museum people waiting for the preview—and a show that the worst gallery in town wouldn't give house room to!

Three of the pictures were called *Empty Carton #1, Empty Carton #2* and *Empty Carton #3*. Gainsborough had fixed actual cardboard cartons to his canvases and, using regular housepaints, had painted in weeds and grasses around them with big, sloppy strokes. All three pictures were exactly alike except for the positions of the boxes. Another, called *Vista,* featured a real window frame with a torn working shade. On another canvas he had dashed off the heads of a crowd of people (and very poorly, too) and glued squares of foam rubber to their foreheads. He called it *The Foam Rubber Culture.* The rest were more of same—terrible. It was pure meanness. The question was why? Had he forgotten how to paint? Did he want to ruin Gregor by making him call off the show? Or did he want him to go on with it and look like a fool? Or did he, perhaps, want Gregor to lose patience and break their contract, setting Gains free to find greener pastures to graze in?

Whatever Gainsborough expected, Gregor went on with the show and, what's more, he got away with it. It was his most brilliant exercise in the psychology of promotion. Somehow he sold it to the press and to the public as Gainsborough Brown's most brutal protest to date against everything that was phony in American art, American culture and in the American people themselves. He said it was a protest born of such anger and despair that the artist scorned to use conventional tools and had cast aside his brilliant technique to speak through the use of pure imagination. They bought the story—all those educated art lovers who ought to have known better—and the exhibition was the biggest smash to date. Lines formed every day an hour before opening time and stretched all around the block. Orders for the catalogue (printed in the utmost haste and finished at the eleventh hour) came in from all over the world, and we had to reorder. There was even an essay on the Op-Ed page of the *Times* examining the role of the artist in today's American Society, calling Gains "an ecological hero."

That was the last show, and it convinced me that Gregor Olitsky could promote anything. It also convinced me that we were in for a bad time in the future, because as far as I was concerned, Gainsborough Brown was just plain lousy.

And now, here we were at last, Gregor and I, about to discover what Gains had wrought.

"We might as well get on with it, Persis. Delay will get us nowhere." Gregor marched forward and put the key in the lock. The door resisted, then swung open. Gregor reached inside and felt for the light switch. He knew that Gains liked strong lighting and that there would be a panel to control big fluorescent ceiling lights. Presently he found it and flicked the bank of switches, causing the murky room to blaze into a lurid, artificial glare. I followed him as he moved inside.

How can I describe the shock that greeted us?

My first impression was that we had intruded on some macabre party. The room was full of grotesque figures and noise—a cacophony of sounds: music, voices, laughter, the whine and stutter of infernal machines. It engulfed us. It assaulted us. It was mad. It sent us reeling together with shock. I had actually started back out the door before I understood that it was a fake. None of it was real. It was the product of Gainsborough's perverted imagination.

What we were looking at was a room full of mannequins, the kind one sees in store windows every day. Except that these had been altered here and there by the application of something, probably polyutherane foam, which changed

51

their shape and made them subtly more human. Strange combinations of clothing covered their bodies, but their faces—in the uncanniest touch of all—had been left absolutely blank. The noise that beat upon us from every side came from tape cartridges fixed to the figures and wired into the electrical system, so that when Gregor switched on the lights, all the tapes had begun to play at once.

Gregor grasped the business about the tapes before I did and went around the room swiftly disconnecting cords while I leaned against the wall and waited for my heart to settle down. No wonder there had been such a fuss about my being present when the studio was opened! I was the only one who had nothing to lose. Either Alida or Gregor might have been tempted to immediately destroy everything here in order to save Gainsborough's reputation, but as a painter myself, I could never let that happen to a fellow artist's work.

After the din had subsided, we both stood very still, only our eyes moving as we looked around and tried to pull ourselves together. Finally Gregor walked over to Gains's worktable, selected a handful of palette knives and slammed them down on the floor as hard as he could. It wasn't much of a gesture, but it seemed to serve.

"There. Nothing much else I can do to get back at him." He ran his fingers through his hair and made a grimace that suddenly turned into a grin. I smiled back at him uncertainly.

"Let's do them one at a time, shall we? I note that each has a title on the pedestal, see?"

"I'll write them down." This was familiar routine, and it snapped the spell. It was our job to do our best for the things in this room no matter what we thought of them personally, for the sake of the artist and now for his wife, to whom this represented his very last legacy.

I took a pad out of my purse and prepared to write down the titles.

There were eight figures, or sculptures, as Gregor later decided to label them. The largest was titled *The Collector,* a squat male form perched atop a four-foot pile of stacked and welded-together beer cans, real cans that had their labels painted out. He was holding a dollhouse in his lap. Gregor switched on the accompanying tape, and we heard a mixture of beer commercials larded with market reports and garbled conversations about art.

There was *Him*—a dedicated athlete hunched over a bicycle. When plugged in, he pedaled furiously in place to the tune of ear-splitting machine noises and electronic sounds. Modern man, I guess.

There was *Her,* his obese mate, sprawled in a chair with a skirt stretched obscenely tight across her flabby thighs. She clutched a telephone, through which rolled a babble of meaningless female conversation. On her head she wore the cap of a real hair dryer, which inflated, as the machine hummed, on command.

A worker called *Labor* leaned against a section of a shiny Cadillac chassis. The tape within disgorged both voices of labor leaders rallying their troops and segments from the old Senate investigations into labor racketeering.

Two figures represented *American Youth.* It was impossible to tell their sex, as both had long hair, trousers, sunglasses and beads. We didn't bother with the tape. Gregor said he was sure it was the terrible music we had heard when we came in.

Social Security was a man holding a golf club like a soldier presenting arms. I recognized his tape as a medley of voices from the recent Republican convention.

A woman reclining in an old chaise longue Gains must have picked off the city dump was named *To the Manor Born.* A ratty feather negligee was wrapped around her, and hundreds upon hundreds of fragments of colored glass were imbedded in her neck, ears and fingers; and when Gregor plugged in the wire, all her false jewels lit up in a blaze of color. For the first time Gregor and I smiled at each other with genuine pleasure because the effect was amusing. But then our smiles froze as we heard the voice on the tape saying, in that unmistakable way, "It's so good of you to come. How nice of you. Do come and sit down and tell me about your work ..." and the voice was that of Aunt Lydie.

"Turn it off!" I cried.

Gregor yanked the plug out of the wall. "The son-of-a-bitch," he said. He spoke with great force; yet for some reason, I had the curious feeling that he wasn't surprised.

I was sick with anger. "How could he do it? How could he? Didn't he know what he was doing, making her look like a fool?"

"Certainly he knew." He was watching me covertly while he fussed around the seedy-looking figure. "And aside from that, what in hell am I supposed to do with this whole mess? He's set the art world back about a thousand years." He made a fist and slammed it into his other palm with a series of sharp smacks. But the way he did it carried no conviction; it was stagey; and suddenly I thought, he doesn't mean it—he's acting! He ought to be more upset. Could he possibly have been here before?

"Look, Persis, we know he was a stupid man. You and I don't have to pretend otherwise. All right." He began to walk back and forth, dodging between the freakish mannequins. "But you tell me how he ever had the unmitigated gall to come up with a show like this. Had he lost his mind? I barely rescued us all from disaster the last time. What in God's name can I do to save this stuff? There's hardly an original idea here, even if it were any good." He stalked up and down some more. "Lawsuits for example. That's all we need. Your aunt is above that, I'm sure."

"She'd ignore it," I agreed with him.

He stopped pacing and relaxed. "I thought so." I had said what he wanted to hear.

"But I wouldn't put *To the Manor Born* on exhibition, Gregor. Not without permission."

He wasn't listening. "We obviously can't destroy this junk or store it away somewhere forever, even if Alida were willing. She seems to have some taste. Because Miss Ives knows it's here and she'd never stand for it. She thinks Gainsborough was God."

He also meant because I'd seen it, too. No matter how ghastly it was, I would consider the destruction of another artist's work to be immoral. And Gains had known that about me, taking advantage of me as he always had.

"No, we can't just bury the work. There's bound to be a stink of some kind. So the problem is, what to do with it. Frankly, Persis, the real problem is how to turn this collection into money."

Gregor strolled over to *The Collector* and ran his hands thoughtfully over the pyramid of beer cans that supported it.

"Rumor, yes. Gossip. That's the answer. Who do these figures represent? Spread the word that each of them represents an important figure. Art. Society. Industry. Labor. Let them speculate. Plant a few names. Stir everybody up." He gave *The Collector* a friendly pat. "I'll call the show Gainsborough Brown's Ugliest Americans: A Devastating Indictment of All the Things He Hated About the Country He Loved; A Great Artist's Last Will and Testament."

He was gaining momentum now. "We'll open the show in Europe. They'll love it. And by the time it gets back here, everybody will be panting to see it. They won't care. . . ."

I had stopped listening. He could go on like this for hours, talking to himself just to see how the ideas sounded. Brainstorming, he called it. I leaned against Gains's worktable and began to sketch. I wanted to remember the room exactly as we had found it. I blocked in a long view of the room, sure that if Gregor noticed what I was doing he would assume that I was making notes. And then I realized that something familiar was missing from the background. Something was different.

"I'll begin right away," Gregor was saying. "Plant a story here and there. A speculation. Nothing concrete . . ."

I studied the room. What was it?

"We'll have posters all over America advertising the show in Europe so that when it gets here . . ."

That was it—posters! They were missing! Gainsborough had always put them up where he was working, his own exhibition posters, from the first to the latest. They were so big and colorful in their heavy frames that I had often wondered how he managed to work beneath their garish competition, even as they fed his ego. Now they were gone—all of them.

"Gregor, the posters are gone!"

He didn't seem surprised. Or wasn't he listening? "Have you checked for signatures, Persis? We're lost if these things aren't signed. No one will believe he really did them."

I hadn't thought to look, but now I went back over everything, checking and making a note of where I found Gainsborough's name on each sculpture because he had signed them in a wild variety of hidden places. I found them concealed on the back of a neck, the inside of a thigh, the top of a head. They bore little resemblance to the neatly stroked name on the Gainsborough Brown paintings because these had been scratched with a penknife, and the effect was scraggly yet oddly triumphant.

While I was searching *To the Manor Born* for a signature, I noticed something I had missed before. It was a crude wooden case pushed into a corner. It rested on small, metal claw feet, like the feet on an old-fashioned bathtub. At first glance I assumed it was just a packing box. Then I went over to examine it.

It was a work in progress. There was a neatly typed title. *Did You Really Think You Could Win?* it said. I lifted the lid. Inside was a mannequin, her limbs neatly arranged as if lying in a coffin. Spooky.

I called to Gregor. "Here's one we missed. He must have just started it. Who do you suppose it was meant to be?"

Gregor came over, and we studied it together. "Maybe it's a 'what,' not a 'who.' Maybe the *Death of Art* or something like that." He brushed it off.

But I continued to stare. Suppose, just suppose, Gainsborough had had a real person in mind, the way he had in the savage satire on Aunt Lydie. He was such a miserable brute, so full of hate and petty cruelty. Suppose he was really involved with another girl—say, the girl at the Whitney, Susan Evans? Suppose this message were meant for Alida. Hadn't Oliver said she had bruises on her arms?

It was a chilling thought.

And the missing posters bothered me. I would have to ask Miss Ives if she knew anything about these. Their absence didn't seem to interest Gregor, probably because they weren't valuable enough.

And Gregor. His behavior bothered me, too. From the time he switched on the lights that started this whole crazy episode, he'd behaved like a man on stage, saying his lines and going through motions.

I was absolutely convinced that he had been here before.

8

Alida had given her permission earlier for the new works to be moved to the gallery that afternoon, and Gregor sent me up to wait in front of the main house so that I could direct the truckers to the studio. He didn't want them pounding on Alida's front door, asking for directions. It took a while, but finally they arrived, with a loud grinding of gears. Together Gregor and I supervised the loading and then followed the van to the gallery, where Mrs. Withers awaited us, wreathed in Aztec-inspired necklaces and whiskey fumes.

"Run out and get us something to eat, will you, Mrs. W.?" Gregor asked her. It was now close to six o'clock. "By the time we get everything unloaded, photographed and catalogued, we'll be too tired to go out to eat."

"Couldn't the move have waited until tomorrow morning? Why pay overtime for these men?" Mrs. W. didn't approve of frivolous expenditures.

"It took us more time at the studio than we had expected. Have a cocktail while you're waiting for the order. We're going to be at this for a while, so there's no hurry." Because Gregor knew she'd have a drink anyway, he thought he'd send her away smiling.

I guess we should have warned her what to expect because when she returned an hour later, her arms laden with cartons of Chinese food, she took one look at Gains's legacy (which by now was scattered around the gallery) and dropped everything she was holding right on the floor. She didn't even notice what she'd done. She just stood there gaping while Gregor and I scrambled around on our knees, picking up our dinner before it could leak out of its containers.

She shook her head a few times as if to clear her vision, then made her pronouncement. "If this is art and if this is what he was fixing up for you, it's a wonder you didn't kill him before he drowned, Mr. Olitsky!"

Having spoken her piece, she lurched off into Gregor's office, where we heard her opening the closet door. There was a long pause. Gregor looked after her. "Gone for another much-needed drink, I guess. Best idea of the day. Shall we?" And he smiled.

I had never been able to resist Gregor's smile and the way it made his neat little moustache jump up and down.

"Fine," I answered, glad of the diversion. Because I didn't want him to guess that I was thinking yes, Mrs. W., you have something there. Any red-blooded art dealer would have wanted to murder an artist who had stuck him with such a lousy show *and* had been up to some unethical hanky-panky, selling paintings behind his dealer's back—or so it seemed. Any dealer, including Gregor.

Except that Gainsborough died while Gregor was still in France, so the whole thing was academic.

My house was ablaze with lights when I arrived home that night. It was about ten thirty. I had stayed on at the gallery after Gregor and Mrs. Withers left to finish developing the photographs of Gains's new work, and I was dead tired.

Damn, I told myself, Mrs. Howard has done it again! Some artist caught her before she left for the day and talked her into letting him wait for me. Why can't she be more hard-hearted? He's probably been dug in for hours, working on my bar and getting ready to unload his troubles on my weary shoulders. Why did I ever get into this business, anyway? And why turn on every light in the house?

I eased the car over the bluestone that made a winding, pebbled path to my front door, driving slowly, ready to slam on the brake if any of the small creatures that inhabited the woods on either side leaped out and was transfixed by my headlights . . . ready to brake hard out of sheer exasperation at the thought of the welcome I would get.

There was a car. Naturally, I expected that. If it was anything special, I didn't notice. With the exception of Aunt Lydie's, all automobiles looked alike to me. Not like paintings.

But there was something out of the ordinary about the man who stepped out of it to greet me. He was Sidney Muss, the collector.

"Mr. Muss!" I didn't quite say what on earth are you doing here, but it hung in the air like a trumpet blast. After all, I'd never spoken to him in my life.

Yet here he was, waving to his chauffeur to get back in the car and walking along beside me, obviously intending to come in. I thought I noticed someone huddled in the back seat as we passed, but I couldn't swear to it because I wasn't really paying attention. Sidney Muss was a natural attention-getter.

"I thought I'd better wait for you, Mrs. Willum. It seemed best," he was saying. "You've had a robbery here." He was maddeningly calm.

"Robbery?" I wasn't sure I'd heard correctly.

"I would have called the police, but I thought you'd prefer to handle it yourself. I'll stay with you until you've had a chance to look around."

I glanced at him to make sure that he wasn't joking, but he wasn't. His face was serious.

"Go in," he told me. "It's perfectly safe. When we found the door open, we went through the house to make sure you weren't inside, injured or something. There's nothing to be afraid of."

And then I forgot about Sidney Muss because we had stepped into the house and it was such a shambles that I just stood still in the hallway, stunned. All I could think of was a cyclone. Or a buffalo stampede. Or a hundred Visigoths on a rampage. Pillage. Destruction. Disaster. I caught my breath, stifling a scream.

The quiet voice behind me was still speaking. "It's not as bad as it looks. All superficial, you'll find. Your studio was the most thoroughly gone over. The rest, I think, is for show."

But I didn't believe it, not a word. With an agonizing effort I forced myself forward, step by step, fighting the impulse to sit down in the midst of everything and blubber like a baby. Upstairs first, with Muss shadowing. Mattresses off beds. Clothes everywhere. Drawers and closets emptied. Rugs turned up. Towels and linens strewn about. Chairs overturned.

The downstairs was more of the same. Kitchen and pantry a disaster area. Every single scrap of paper and canvas in the porch that doubled as my studio, out of place and scattered. All the pictures, off the walls and dumped on the floor. Books tumbled off the shelves.

"They forced their way in through that screen, you'll notice. Left through the front door, of course." I was surprised to find he was still with me. Because I couldn't think of anything else to do, I bent over, picked up an armload of books and began to replace them. Picked up some more books. Put them away. And some more. Like a machine that once set in motion goes on interminably, I found myself stooping, gathering and reshelving over and over again.

Muss was at my bar. "I believe you could use a drink. I'll fix it. Brandy, I think." I could hear him making the familiar noises ... a bottle unstoppered ... a clink of glass ... the gurgle of liquid. "Do stop for a second and drink this. It will do you good." The voice was impersonal but the words had a kind ring, and I was grateful. He righted a chair, and I sat down on it and took the glass he handed me I sat down because I didn't want to be standing there, taller than he. I don't imagine Muss would have cared. If size was his hang-up, he must have mastered it, along with just about everything else, long ago. But suddenly I wanted to do something nice for him to reciprocate and it was all I could think of.

He had made himself a drink, too, and faced me with it in his hand. "The thing to do, Mrs. Willum, is to make a mental inventory right now. Can you think of anything that's missing?"

I didn't want to look at him because then I would have to do as he asked. I would have to pull myself together and I wasn't ready. I stared distractedly around the room, wondering how long it would take to restore to it a semblance of order. I swallowed some brandy, twirling the glass in my hand. I began to picture the internal course of the hot liquid through my body and tried to guess how soon I would feel its effect. I studied the left ear of Sidney Muss with great concentration—it was just an ear—and finally, in desperation, the soft, expensive leather of his highly polished shoes. He had very big feet. A small man with very big feet. What did that make him? I tried to think about that for a while. But nothing helped.

Muss spoke. "What about jewels—all there?" I nodded. They had all seemed to be there—what there was of them. "Silver? Appliances? Television? Money? Any other valuables—all there?" I nodded again, doing an inventory in spite of myself. I hadn't noticed anything—anything of importance, that is—missing. Except . . . could it be possible? I stared at the library window seat. The top was up. The window seat had been emptied.

"You see," Muss was saying, in his careful way, "I have a theory they were after pictures because of the way they went through your studio. Do you have any stashed away—Gainsborough Browns, for instance? I'm sure this wasn't an ordinary thief; he was looking for something special."

"No," I said, "no pictures. The only Browns I have are right on the wall in the other room, and they're all right—

all there and all right. There isn't anything else. Just my own work and a few other things . . . nothing important or valuable."

I was sure now what they had been after—Gainsborough's wooden box. And they had it. It was gone. But I was puzzled. Why, if someone broke into my house to get it, would he take the time and trouble to go through all the rest of the rooms wreaking such havoc when the box must have been one of the very first things he found after he came through the window? Was the thief really after something else? Something more? No, that couldn't be. There was nothing else in my house to steal. Certainly no Gainsborough Browns except the ones I'd owned forever that were right in sight.

"Well," said the collector, "I should be on my way, now that I know you're all right. I had wanted to talk to you, but this may not be the time." However, he made no move to go and I realized that he had no intention of leaving. As considerate as he had been these last few minutes, he now gave the impression of asking in return my full attention; and I had no choice but to give it to him, out of a sense of obligation.

"Why did you come to see me tonight, Mr. Muss?"

"I have been thinking of it for some time. I want to make you a business proposition."

A faint curiosity stirred within me. "Yes?"

"I came to ask you how you'd like to make fifteen thousand dollars for yourself, Mrs. Willum."

"Fifteen thousand dollars?" I echoed, unbelieving.

"I know you could use the money. You are not very well off. You see, I've had you investigated quite thoroughly. Don't take offense. It's my way whenever I'm doing business." I didn't take offense. I was too astounded. Furthermore, he spoke so impersonally that I couldn't really believe he was talking about me.

"All you have to do is to persuade Mrs. Gainsborough Brown to sell me the contents of her husband's studio at the time of his death. I will pay whatever you think fair.

You have a reputation for absolute honesty."

It took a minute for the full meaning of his proposition to hit me. He was asking me to accept a personal commission on what should be a gallery sale. Surely he must know—everyone knew—that Gregor Olitsky and his gallery were Gainsborough's agents?

"But, Mr. Muss, the gallery . . . Gregor Olitsky . . ."

He understood me well enough. "I will not deal with Olitsky. What Mrs. Brown does about the gallery commission is her affair and yours. I have said I'll pay your price. But I want my name kept out of it until the transaction is complete. Olitsky is not to know." I tried to read his eyes. They were as expressive as two stones.

"I couldn't possibly . . ." I began.

He held up his hand. "No, no more discussion. Don't answer now. Sleep on it. You'll see that there's no harm in my proposition when you've had a chance to think about it. Call me tomorrow. I'll be at my apartment in town." And then, intensely, "Mrs. Willum, have you any so-called friend who might wish you ill?"

It was such an archaic way of putting it that I almost smiled and congratulated him on changing the subject so brilliantly. Almost—until I thought of Gregor. His name crept into my mind unwelcome and unbidden. Gregor was my friend . . . correction: had been my friend. More than a friend, really; a father figure who had given me a job I loved, an interest in life and countless good times and good advice. Until Paris. Was he still my friend?

"Do you remember a movie called *Suspicion?* The heroine was portrayed like a forest animal—afraid of the hunter but waiting for him, too. I've seen it many times, watching her wait for the hunter to stalk, to kill. You may find yourself acquiring something of that same quality, Mrs. Willum, the same look . . ."

The thought crossed my mind that he might be joking, but I dismissed it. He didn't get where he was today making meaningless jokes in bad taste.

"Are you saying that someone is stalking me, Mr. Muss?"

I shouldn't have said it, it broke the spell.

"Did I say that?" He turned away and very carefully placed his glass on the bar. "I must go now." He brushed past me, with a polite nod, and walked briskly out of the library, through the living room to my front hall. I followed a few steps behind like a respectful lackey, wishing I could think of something useful to say. At the door I offered my hand, but he rejected it. I even imagined I saw a flash of distaste, as if the thought of touching my flesh repelled him. He presented a stiff little bow, and then, like a man who had overlooked something important, drew a piece of rolled paper out of his pocket. "I meant to give this to you at once," he told me. "Sometimes I am very forgetful."

I saw the jagged edges where the sheet had been separated from the sketchbook, and I knew what I would see even before I unrolled it—the sketch of Gainsborough Brown's murder at the edge of the pool.

"Your notebook was on the floor open to that page when I came in. Burn it, Mrs. Willum. Tear it into a million pieces. Destroy it at once. If you've accidentally or on purpose illustrated the truth, you may have put your life in jeopardy."

Now he was going down the steps. The chauffeur had jumped out of the front seat and was sprinting around to open the door before Muss got there. Unfortunately, the collector had one more ominous thing to say to me.

"And watch out for Olitsky, Mrs. Willum. Don't trust him!"

The car door swung wider and Muss stepped in. I caught the briefest glimpse of another person—a girl?—in the back seat. Then the door closed smartly.

9

When he had gone, I began a second search of the house just to make sure that I was correct and that nothing else was missing.

It was a strange experience in some ways. Objects kept floating to the surface and taking me by surprise, like attending an octogenarian meeting or recognizing a childhood friend in the line at the Radio City Music Hall. Here was the snakeskin walking stick Aunt Lydie had sent me from India the year I broke my leg skiing on a college weekend. How snappy I'd felt when I was out of the cast and able to use it. Here was the water bowl of the late, great Caesar, the noble dog I had never replaced because he was irreplaceable. Mrs. Howard had stored it with the best silver, carefully wrapped in brown paper and labeled "Ceezar" in her handwriting. Infallible taste on her part. Anything of Caesar's belonged with the family treasures. There were old letters from forgotten artists. Catalogues from forgotten shows. A crumpled tie from the sometimes-forgotten husband, whose shadow never quite dissipated. How had Mrs. Howard and I missed it? Everything of his had been banished long ago.

Things like that—hundreds of them—each clamoring for attention until I felt that I was trying to wade through an endless sea of memorabilia, the bits and pieces clinging stubbornly to my legs and making progress quite impossible.

But I plowed resolutely ahead. There was no other way I could think of to be absolutely certain that only Gainsborough's box was missing. A knife-edge of pain sliced into the small of my back. My eyes began to give me trouble, protesting lids threatening to close in spite of me. I spent more and more of my time looking at things while sitting down, and it became more and more of an effort to get up again.

Finally I was finished. Bent over and stiff, but finished.

Nothing was missing except the box. Yet it didn't make sense. Or did it? There was nothing that had seemed to me to be of any significance in the box, certainly nothing to warrant the havoc wreaked among my belongings. Was I wrong? I was just too tired to reexamine my conclusions and had to marshal all my strength in order to scrawl a note to Mrs. Howard.

Dear Mrs. H:

I hate leaving you such a pigpen. Maybe a match would cure it. Can you think of anyone who has been here or anything unusual that has happened in the last couple of months? Anything at all—workmen, repairs, deliveries, etc. Thanks.

P.W.

After that I tumbled into bed, wrapping a pillow around each ear as usual and winding my arms around them to keep them in place. Then I fell asleep.

I must have been in the deepest trough of slumber when the telephone began to ring. For a long time I thought it was part of a dream. As nearly as I could remember the next day the conversation, when I finally lifted the receiver, went like this:

"Mrs. Willum? It's Susan Evans. Forgive me for calling so late." She was whispering.

"Yes."

"Could I come to see you tomorrow night? I'm afraid it

will have to be late. Maybe after midnight."

"All right."

"And thank you. Thank you for not telling. . . ."

The connection was broken in mid-sentence, I think. I got the receiver back on the hook somehow and went on sleeping.

I was in the car and away early the next morning. I had reached an important decision: I could not be passive; I would have to act. And I was about to take my first step.

The eight o'clock traffic was not too bad, at least it was moving swiftly, and I skimmed along the Expressway and onto the Cross Island with no interruptions. It promised to be a beautiful day. The sailboats on the Sound rocked and swayed on the dancing waters. By eight forty-five I was soaring over the Throgs Neck Bridge, and even in my anxiety and fatigue I marveled once again that such a lovely structure could have been saddled with such an uninspiring name.

It took a little over an hour from the bridge to reach my destination. I had to stop to ask directions once and once I almost made a wrong turn, but I felt, all in all, that I was making good time. It was a few minutes after ten when I pulled into the town of Briarcliff Manor. Five minutes later I stopped at the address I was looking for—a white clapboard house that looked like a million other small-town houses in the United States. It was a vertical box on a narrow lot, its spindling front porch surrounded by spirea bushes and shaded by a single maple tree. A cement walk with grass growing between the cracks led down to the sidewalk. Even the address sounded right—14 Maple Street.

I took a deep breath and pressed the doorbell.

Though I couldn't see through the screened door, I heard the bell shrill deep inside the house and presently there were footsteps and a voice calling, "Don't go away. I'm coming." When she materialized on the other side of the door, the woman didn't seem particularly surprised to

68

see me. "What can I do for you?"

This was the important moment. "Hello, I'm Persis Willum. I hope I'm not . . . I know I'm probably a few minutes late." It was the first thing that came into my head. I hadn't known what I was going to say. Now it was her turn.

She looked puzzled, but just for an instant. Then her frown vanished as a naturally friendly disposition took command, and she motioned me into the house. "Mrs. Brown didn't say anything about expecting you, but she probably forgot. She's off to the doctor again. I'm Jane Milliken from down the street. I'm keeping an eye on her washing machine for her—it suddenly decided to go crazy and you have to watch it every minute. Really! Too bad the poor thing can't get a new one, but with a husband like that and her having to work, I suppose she has to get along with what she has."

I was dying to pick up the thread she'd dropped about the "husband like that" and ask a few little questions. Instead: "You said the doctor—is she ill?"

"Doesn't seem so, but I don't know anything about it. She's not a talker. All I know is that she comes up once in a while in the middle of the week, but generally she's only here weekends. Trying to keep this house up in case she ever gets her husband back. Personally, I don't think she will if it's a war disability like people say. Get him back, I mean. Not likely." There was a sudden ominous noise from the back regions of the house. "My God—the machine—blast off! Excuse me and make yourself comfortable. She ought to be back in a minute." Mrs. Milliken fled. I thought of following her to see what more she would tell me—she seemed an enthusiastic talker—but the roars of the washing machine intimidated me, and I decided that Mrs. Milliken was probably too occupied for idle chatter. To my right was a bay-windowed sitting room. I went in, moved some magazines off a chair and sat down. The chair was worn, the magazines out of date.

I amused myself by trying to guess from the character of

the room what its mistress would be like. Greyish walls in need of paint . . . furniture with the scruffy look of having been secondhand to begin with . . . some dried flowers . . . a few dreary dime store reproductions of Currier and Ives. All that came to mind was an impersonal second-string motel room.

It was very quiet on Maple Street. I could hear a squirrel chattering away in a nearby tree and, ever so faintly, the sound of a vacuum cleaner humming to itself in the house next door. I even caught the occasional cries of children in a playground I had passed several blocks away. Friendly sounds, all of them. Encouraging. Saying, it seemed to me, that I would be lucky.

The washing machine must have settled down because everything was so quiet. Perhaps now I should go back and talk to Mrs. Milliken. But even as I considered it a car swirled into the driveway and around toward the back of the house. A door slammed. Mrs. Milliken called out and there was a brief conversation. The car went away again. Then light footsteps coming slowly down the hall.

"You wanted to see me?"

A woman was standing in the doorway. I suppose that with the sunlight streaming in the window behind me directly into her eyes, she couldn't have been expected to recognize me instantly. I know that I didn't recognize her. But after all, I had never seen her with her hair brushed and hanging free. I had never seen her with lipstick on, even so pale a lipstick. I had never seen her in a decent dress. And most of all, I had never seen her without her glasses. I realized in those few seconds that—in spite of my artist's eye—I had never really known what she looked like. And yet standing before me was Hope Ives!

"Miss Ives, it's me, Persis Willum." She hadn't recognized me yet, I could tell, because she hadn't moved. Unlike me. I think I must have jumped a foot when I realized who she was. "I didn't expect it to be anyone I knew, least of all you," I was babbling along, not really caring if I made sense, feeling like someone in a form of shock. "I suppose I should call you Mrs. Brown?"

"Mrs. Willum. Dear Heaven!" She understood finally. "Oh, no!"

She stood very still, all color washed from her face, her breathing suddenly rapid and shallow. Like a blind person, she felt for a chair and sat down. She looked so terrible that I felt guilty, as if I had deliberately caused her pain.

"I never expected it to be you," I repeated.

"H-how did you guess?" Her voice was faint.

"I saw an old photograph among Gainsborough's things. A snapshot of a girl I didn't know, and I wondered if it could be Gainsborough's first wife."

We looked at one another. I had the crazy illusion that I could hear both our hearts pounding in unison. I forced myself to go on. "I remember where Gainsborough came from, so I took a chance and asked Information for Oscar Brown on School Street—most towns have a School Street— and Information said, no, but she had a Mrs. O. Brown on Maple Street."

She was so pale. "As easy as that!"

"Yes. I just happened to think of it, that's all."

"But why? Why did you care about the first Mrs. Brown?"

"I don't really know. Gains has been so on my mind, and I wanted to begin at the beginning."

"I see." She paused. "After all I've done, after all the lies I've lived, as easy as that. The beginning. How I wish we were at the beginning again. I'd do so many things differently." She had been fumbling in the pocket of her skirt. Finally she found a cigarette. "Have you a match? Oh, thanks." When I gave her the matches both our hands were shaking. She made a great business of lighting the cigarette and, without inhaling, blew several large nervous puffs of smoke before speaking again.

"Yes, if I had another chance I'd do it all so differently. I haven't been smart, haven't done one thing right from the very start." She made a gesture of despair. "Mrs. Willum,

I'm *still* his wife. I'm still Mrs. Gainsborough Brown. We were never divorced."

The squirrel began to chatter again outside the window, scolding, scolding. "Never divorced, never divorced," he complained crossly. The whole room tilted slightly on its axis and the sunlight on my back was a physical thing—heavy, like a weight.

"Never divorced," I whispered.

"That's right. You know how he was. I don't have to tell you, of all people. He wanted the whole cake, not just a piece. And no strings. He wanted to be free to seize every opportunity as it presented itself. Free to come and go, to climb, to be important."

"I know. Free to win the ballgame."

"But he couldn't just kick me out. It wasn't that easy. Because he needed me." She laughed a little but there was no humor in it. "I mean really needed me. You see, I was teaching art in grade school when I married Gains, and I thought fooling around with painting would be something to amuse him when he was between jobs. He was so often between jobs, and you know how unpleasant he could be when he was depressed."

Indeed, I did know how unpleasant he could be. I could imagine her struggling to find any pastime that would keep him occupied and soothe his ego.

"Anyway," she continued, still smiling that grim smile, "I kept on working because we had to eat, and he'd sit home all day and paint. At night I'd criticize his things and try to encourage him. You can imagine that it was more encouragement than criticism. Gainsborough didn't like criticism of any kind, did he? He showed, in time, a little ability; but I honestly didn't even consider him good enough for the little local shows, and you know how awful they are. But he was crazy to have someone other than me admire him, and one day he announced that he was taking his paintings and going to New York. I didn't object. How could I? Let him get it out of his system, I thought. He'll be back with his tail between his legs. But I didn't hear from him for over a month, and I got worried. I was afraid he might have left me, that the whole thing was just an excuse. I always worried that he might leave me. And then a bill arrived from a Madison Avenue framer for nine hundred dollars. And can you believe that I was happy to get it, although nine hundred dollars was a fortune to me, because it meant he hadn't left me?"

She looked at me appealingly.

"What did you do?" There was a horrid fascination to her revelations, and I wanted her to go on.

"I took the next train to New York and went straight to the framer. There they were—all of Gainsborough's pictures—as beautifully framed as if we were millionaires. I must say, they looked somewhat better in the frames. I paid as much as I could. The firm was very nice and let me pay for the rest on time. They were used to artists and their problems. And they told me where I could find Gains." She put her hands over her eyes. "He looked awful, Mrs. Willum. I'll never forget! I finally tracked him down in the most miserable, flea-bitten hotel you could imagine on West Forty-third Street. I should have left him then while there was still time. But he was so thin and dirty and he'd grown that miserable scraggly beard—remember?—that I just loved him more. He told me he had to stay in New York. He was going to be in a show with you, he said, and it was his big chance—*our* big chance. I still didn't believe he'd make it. As far as I was concerned, he was strictly no-talent and he'd come back to me soon. I believed it because it's the way I wanted it. So I said good luck and went home and went back to work. You know the rest."

I thought I could guess the next part. "He sold a couple of pictures and then wild horses couldn't drag him out of New York. He kept you out of sight while he made contacts and sold pictures, I know that. And his work improved. But then what happened?"

"He asked for a divorce. He said quite frankly that he'd outgrown me. He told me I wasn't a social asset. I think he had visions of making an important marriage some day. He was very definite. He must have a divorce. I said I'd think about it, although I never intended to agree, not after all I'd put up with to keep our marriage intact! Instead, I went away for three months, and while I was gone he began some new canvases and found he couldn't paint a lick without me. He just had no imagination. No taste. He couldn't even understand what to put in and what to leave out.

"So he found out he needed me, and we worked out a compromise. He would say he was divorced for the sake of furthering his career, and I would tell everyone up here that my husband was in a veterans' hospital and that I was working in New York to be near him. Actually, I was living with him as his secretary."

"How could you agree to that? It must have been awful for you." I had to know.

She seemed surprised that I would ask. "But it wasn't so bad, really. We were together. It was better than nothing, better than letting someone else have him. No matter where he went or what he did or whom he did it with, he was still mine."

I couldn't help remembering what Oliver had said about Alida the night of Aunt Lydie's party: "Who can explain love?" What was there about Gains to inspire the love of two nice women like Alida and Hope Ives? His glowering animal good looks? His belief in his own genius? His cruelty? And had he loved either of them in return?

Miss Ives knew what I was thinking. "I never knew whether he loved me. But he loved the power I gave him . . ." Her voice trailed off.

"What about his last work—all those strange figures?"

Her whole face changed and closed. "I had nothing to do with it." I waited for her to go on, but she didn't.

"He was married to Alida by then, wasn't he? Forgive my asking, but how could he marry her if you were never divorced? I don't understand."

She shuddered. "I wanted to kill myself at first. I had to face the fact that there wasn't anything he wouldn't stoop to. Do you know, he expected me just to go away and leave

74

him to live with Alida. I was to say nothing, cause no trouble. It was the 'decent' thing to do, he said. Can you imagine? This time I think he meant it, that we were through. I hung on anyway, still fighting to keep my marriage. I was his legal wife, after all."

"Did you tell him that?"

"Of course. And he got so ugly that for a few days it was like living in the mouth of a cannon. He was trying to get me to leave out of sheer misery. Finally I couldn't stand it any longer and I threatened to expose him to the press. Then he changed his tune at once. This marriage to Alida was going to make him a fortune, he said, and he would share it with me. So I was just to hang on and keep quiet."

"I see." Was there anyone living who didn't have a good reason to murder Gainsborough Brown? Certainly I wouldn't blame Miss Ives if she'd pushed him into the pool that night. It must have occurred to her that if Gainsborough Brown found himself with a fortune on his hands, he would never paint again, being the lazy lout he was. And if he never painted again, he would have no further need of her. In fact, he had already prepared his last show without her help. A show with a "corpse" in a coffin that undoubtedly represented his resentment against a woman in his life whom he would just as soon . . .

Just then she did something I was to recall afterward as being a strange thing to do, although at the time it touched me as an odd little gesture of vanity. She drew a pair of glasses from her pocket and pressed them into my hand. "Look through them," she urged. I did. They were as clear as window glass. "I don't need glasses any more than you do," she told me. "You see? I started wearing them when I came to live with Gains as his secretary to make sure no one would recognize me as the first Mrs. Brown. Gainsborough hated me in them. I had to take them off the minute we were alone. But they worked. No one ever recognized me or suspected that we were anything but employer and secretary."

It must have been hard for her, when Gains made no

secret of the fact that he found girls who wore glasses sexless and dull.

"So don't give me away now, please," she was saying as we moved together toward the door. "I've had all the pain I can stand. And it would hurt her, Alida. I suppose she has to be considered. She must have loved him, too."

"I won't say anything," I promised, hoping it was a promise I would be able to keep. "But I don't understand why the newspapers never got to you after Gains died. They must have tried to track you down."

"I guess they must have, but Gains had taken great pains to obliterate all links to the past. You know how he revelled in being a mysterious figure. You knew more about him than anyone else, but if a reporter had asked you about his first wife, you couldn't have told them anything, could you?"

I admitted that she was right. I thought of something else, something that didn't make sense. "Miss Ives, could it be possible that Gainsborough didn't tell you the truth about why he married Alida? Could it have been for some reason other than money? She seems to have so little of it, after all. That house is absolutely threadbare, and there's only Maggie to look after things."

Miss Ives reacted swiftly. "I never said that *she* had money, did I? That wasn't it. I said the marriage would bring him a lot of money, that's the way he put it. You know how he talked. And I'm sure he meant it because he started right in to hire servants and fix up the house."

"Well, he stopped pretty quickly, didn't he? What happened? How could the marriage make him rich if she didn't have money?" I was moving toward the porch, I needed the air.

There was a slight hesitation, then she said, "I suggest that you ask your aunt about that."

What could Lydia Wentworth know about Gains's second marriage? How could I ever ask her such a question? While I was still trying to gather my scattered wits, the screened door closed politely but firmly in my face.

10

I was almost past the White Plains cut-off and on the New England Thruway on my way home before I realized that I was being followed. It was a wonder I noticed at all. I'm a vague driver at best; and after what I had just been through, I was more than usually distracted. But the green sedan hung there on the periphery of my consciousness, dogging me with relentless persistence until I couldn't help but notice, particularly since the traffic was light.When I slowed down, it slowed down. When I changed lanes, it changed lanes. When I made a mistake and started to turn off at the wrong exit, it made the same mistake and swung back into the traffic with me like a green shadow.

It was a novel sensation. I had never been followed by a car before—at least not since I was a young girl and attracted the regulation number of teenage admirers on wheels. And I had the queerest feeling that I could have been followed since I left my house this morning and never noticed until now. There had been too much traffic on the way up. Now, among the thinning cars, it was obvious.

We were approaching the point where I would normally move into the left lane to take the route to the Throgs Neck Bridge and back to Long Island. Instead, I turned toward New York City and was shortly engulfed in the city traffic. I could see my uninvited escort behind me, joining the snakelike procession in which we moved uptown, rolling through the congestion like two logs in a jam. We couldn't have lost one another if we'd tried!

I didn't try. What I did was to turn in to the first garage I came to that wasn't sporting a FULL sign. I seized my ticket from the startled attendant, and sprinted down the block in search of a cab. I finally had to go right out in the street and flag one down. "Nineteen East Sixty-fourth Street." It was all I could think of doing. If my shadow could manage to get another taxi fast enough to follow me, why, let him. He would find me doing what I would normally do for part of the day when I'm in the city—check out the gallery shows and do the museums and special exhibitions.

All the way downtown I resisted the impulse to look out the window to see if we were being followed. I wouldn't do it normally, so I couldn't do it now. And as I stepped out in front of Wildenstein, I looked neither right or left. It was an effort, but I managed it.

The girl behind the desk smiled at me as I came in. "Good afternoon, Mrs. Willum. Nice to see you. You'll like the show today. It's a benefit for Cancer Care."

I moved toward the covey of ladies that surrounded a table near the elevator to the main exhibition room. They were the volunteers collecting entrance fees. I presented my money, handed over an additional sum for a catalogue and was allowed to pass.

The rooms were jammed—no question about the success of this presentation. There was also the usual collection of well-dressed women and a number of affluent-looking men who had stopped by on their way to a late lunch. There were arty types, too, and many students. I noticed one group of teenage boys in school blazers—a refreshingly neat platoon studying the pictures under the guidance of an instructor who didn't look any older than his charges. Around this little nucleus swirled other viewers, getting in on the lecture. They had their catalogues unfurled and their eyes fixed firmly on the walls.

I moved slowly around the rooms, pretending at first to study the pictures and finally becoming totally involved in

78

them. It was quite impossible to give them mere cursory attention. They were too beautiful. Some were familiar to me through other loan exhibitions of the past, but a few were masterpieces I had never seen before, except in reproduction. There was a glowing Renoir of his son Jean with Gabrielle Renard, one of Renoir's favorite models. There was a charming Mary Cassatt. A shimmering Pissarro. An early Monet which, my catalogue informed me, had never been exhibited in the fifty years it had remained in one private collection. What a shame, I thought, that my aunt never lent her pictures on an occasion like this. Any one of them would have enhanced this exhibition, splendid though it was.

And then I saw that there was one person here who was not looking at pictures. He was moving along with everyone else, holding a catalogue, but he wasn't *looking;* he wasn't even looking at me. He was there, a few discreet steps away, wherever I went, and I knew that I was still being followed.

I think my main reaction was anger. I don't know why. I guess I was too tired and hungry to feel anything else. And, in addition, I just naturally assumed that the whole thing was due to Sidney Muss and his mania for having people investigated when he was planning to do business with them. So I did what could have turned out to be a very foolish thing. I squeezed in among the young students and told their instructor, "That man over there is going to slash one of these pictures. I saw the knife in his hand. Could you see that he doesn't get out of here while I go and get the management?"

Things happened very quickly then. The man was surrounded and pinned against the wall before he could object, lost from sight behind a screen of athletic young males, while all the other people in the gallery milled about and screamed delicately. I didn't wait. While the ladies at the admission table were still rising from their seats, twittering with alarm, I left. Whatever occurred next, I was sure that it would be a good while before my shadow could extricate himself.

I headed for Madison Avenue. It was where I'd intended to go in the beginning, the offices of Miss Styles, Aunt Lydie's secretary.

Miss Styles had been Aunt Lydie's secretary forever, which is to say roughly forty years. She had taken the job in the days when a young and glamorous Miss Wentworth needed her only to keep track of her social engagements, pay her bills and see that she answered her mail. But as the years went by and Aunt Lydie's affairs became more involved, Miss Styles acquired a secretary of her own over whom she presided with a certain grandeur. She had also acquired the habit of identifying completely with her employer: "We will be at the Court Tennis this weekend." she would say, or "We will have to regret that invitation. We are attending a ball."

The *under* secretary was alone in the outer office when I came in. She barely glanced at me before she went back to her typing. "Good afternoon, Mrs. Willum. Miss Styles is in conference. Won't you sit down and wait?"

In conference—pretty grand, I thought. I looked for a place to sit down and finally selected the chair behind Miss Styles's desk. Actually, there wasn't any other place to sit. Everything was stacked with packages and boxes from what must have been every store in New York. I wondered if my aunt had done her Christmas shopping early and if it had all been delivered at once.

The door to the second room was closed. This was the room Aunt Lydie reserved for herself when she came in to go over correspondence and accounts with Miss Styles. Whatever conference was going on in there now must be too important for the undersecretary's ears.

The desk behind which I was sitting looked like it had sustained a direct hit from a bomb. A couple of layers of scattered papers covered the surface—letters, bills, receipts, invitations, telegrams, art catalogues, advertising fliers. Since Miss Styles was generally a model of neatness and order, there could be only one explanation: She must be in the process of gathering together for mailing all the odds and ends which she thought would interest my aunt. Bulging manila envelopes went off to her once or twice a week when she was abroad, and Aunt Lydie looked forward to their arrival as eagerly as any early settler in this country ever looked forward to the arrival of the pony express.

One piece of paper in particular attracted my attention because it was on top of the litter and had an attached memo on which Miss Styles had written with her usual flourish of exclamation marks: HIGHEST PRIORITY!!!!! Please select sample of new monogramming IF YOU WANT IT and return POST HASTE. TIME OF ESSENCE!!!!!

There had been a low, off-and-on hum of conversation from the inner office. Now the door opened and, to my astonishment, Gregor came out, followed by Miss Styles. I'm not sure which of us was the most surprised. Perhaps they were because they both gazed at me with the most unusual expression, as if they were guilty of something and had been caught.

"Hello, Gregor," I said.

"Why, Persis, what are you doing here?" He didn't sound pleased.

"I was meeting someone for lunch, but the plans got changed." It was a small fib.

"Well, it's too bad you didn't let me know. You could have driven in with me. Lydia asked me to check up on some pictures she's having cleaned, and I'm just reporting in to Miss Styles." Behind closed doors? I doubted it. He must be looking for Aunt Lydie.

Gregor changed the subject. "I just checked in with Withers and she says Sidney Muss has been trying to reach you all day. She gave me the number in case I talked to you. I didn't know you and he were such good friends."

"We aren't. He was at Aunt Lydie's party. But, of course, you weren't there, were you?" I copied the number from his notebook into mine. Muss would be calling to see if I was accepting his offer. He hadn't received my note of refusal yet. I hadn't had the guts to do it over the phone.

"What does he want with you then?"

Miss Styles interrupted. "Maybe he wants to invite her to dinner, Mr. Olitsky." For a maiden lady of advancing years, she was amazingly romantic.

"No. He wouldn't ask her to call back. It must be something else. Why don't you call him, Persis? I'm curious."

Aunt Lydie's secretary giggled nervously. She was so tall and angular and spare of frame that it was like seeing a giraffe in the throes of girlish mirth. So I mustered a laugh myself. "No, I don't think I will. He can try me again if he didn't care to leave a message. I'm certainly not going to call him now." Should I tell Gregor about Muss's proposition? No, better to say nothing.

Gregor didn't like it, but he let it go. And after a few pleasantries he bowed to all of us, including the under-secretary, who blushed with pleasure, and left us. When the door had closed, Miss Styles and her assistant sighed. "What a handsome man," they said in unison. Gregor always had that effect on women.

Miss Styles was the first to collect herself. "And now, Mrs. Willum, what can we do for you?"

"It's about my aunt, Miss Styles. I know she left for Paris the day of Gains's funeral, but I've been trying to get in touch with her and I can't reach her at any of the usual places. She's not registered at the Meurice, the Ritz, the Crillon or the George the Fifth. Where in the world has she disappeared to?"

I couldn't interpret Miss Styles's expression. Was it chagrin? "I know," she murmured. "Everyone's looking for her."

"But you must know where she is, Miss Styles. You must. You always do."

"Well, I don't. She telephones here once a week, and I send her mail care of American Express."

"Are you sure she's in Paris at all? Maybe she never went. Maybe she's right here somewhere, trying to avoid all the publicity about Gainsborough Brown's death."

"Oh, no, it isn't that, although we do dislike publicity, as you know. So unattractive." She pursed her lips and rattled her tight grey curls back and forth disapprovingly. The undersecretary stopped typing for a beat and shook her head, too. Publicity was a naughty word in this office.

I was baffled. Plainly my aunt's faithful old Girl Friday wasn't going to give me any information. Didn't she know where Aunt Lydie was, or was she just not telling? I tried another subject. "Do you know if she saw Gainsborough Brown any time before he died?"

This time she didn't mind talking. "I'm afraid she did, alas. I made several appointments for him to visit us at The Crossing. In late June, as I recall. It was odd because he wasn't a favorite of ours. Not our type at all."

"Have you any idea what it was about?"

"No, Mrs. Willum. I can't imagine."

"Oh." Could Gains have been using *To the Manor Born* to blackmail my aunt? And what about Sidney Muss? Wasn't it probable that Gains was also trying to blackmail him with *The Collector*—that squat figure, those beer cans? One thing, though. While Muss might have something to hide, my aunt certainly didn't. And it wouldn't have taken several visits to settle the matter. Five minutes would have been enough. My aunt could be tough when she had to be!

The telephone on the desk rang suddenly. Miss Styles excused herself and picked it up. She listened for a moment, then said, "Just a minute, please. I wish to take this on another line." She put the telephone down on the desk and went into Aunt Lydie's private room to use the extension. The abandoned instrument lay within inches of my fingers. The undersecretary had her back to me. I knew that I was going to listen in. This might be the weekly call from Paris!

But, of course, Miss Styles came back. I might have known she would. She replaced the telephone on its cradle and returned to the other room, closing the door behind her. I listened quite frankly, but I couldn't hear much. She might have been having trouble with the overseas connection, as her voice rose now and again. But most of her side of the conversation was conducted in a guarded mumble. Once I thought I heard her say, "Mr. Olitsky is worried sick," but I wasn't sure.

When she emerged, she had a strangely triumphant air. "I'm sorry I haven't been of any help to you, Mrs. Willum. Perhaps she'll write you. And I'll surely tell her next time she calls that you're anxious to get in touch with her."

"I wish you would. I'm really alarmed about her disappearance."

"Alarmed?" Miss Styles allowed herself a trilling laugh, a good imitation of my aunt's. "You young people. You think everyone older than you has one foot in the grave. Well, we're not dead yet, don't you worry. No, indeed, not yet. Haven't you ever heard of vintage wines?"

"I didn't say anything about being old, Miss Styles. I want to be sure she's all right, that's all. By the way, what pictures is Miss Wentworth having cleaned?"

"Cleaned? I don't know of any." Then she remembered. "Oh, you mean the ones Mr. Olitsky is taking care of? I don't know. I'll have to look them up."

I said good-bye to her very politely because I didn't want her to guess that I no longer needed to know where Aunt Lydie was. While I was sitting at Miss Styles's desk waiting for her to finish the telephone call, I had idly opened the desk drawer and there they were—a neat stack of brown envelopes, waiting to be filled with the selected items of interest and sent on to my aunt. The one on top was already stamped and addressed, not to American Express but to an address I had never seen before, on the Avenue Raphaël in the 16th Arrondissement.

I now knew where my aunt was hiding, but I still didn't know why. Never mind. I would call her as soon as I got home.

11

I remember the beginning of the evening that followed, of course, and I remember the fun part well enough. But the ending was something else again. There were times when I thought I might have dreamed it.

It began with finding Gregor, together with his car and driver, waiting when I stepped out of Aunt Lydie's office. He wore a smile that indicated that if he had been displeased with me a few minutes ago, he had now forgiven me for whatever it was.

"Ahoy," Gregor said. "Like a lift?" It was the hour when cabs were hardest to get. Every block in the area would be dotted with would-be taxi fares, most of whom would still be standing there for some time to come.

"Even if you're lucky enough to stop a cab, you don't want to drive yourself home, Persis. It's rush hour, bumper-to-bumper time. Why not give Bennett here your ticket," Gregor wheedled. "We'll swing past your garage, wherever it is, and let him pick up your car and drive it out. You can loaf in comfort with me at the wheel."

"Be glad to, Mrs. Willum," Bennett said. "No trouble."

I hesitated only a second, just long enough to watch two men in the street trying in vain to stop a rushing taxi. Then I hopped in beside Gregor.

Why wasn't I more suspicious of his sudden change of humor after his recent attempts to keep me at arm's length? Because I didn't want to be, obviously. I longed for the old camaraderie I associated with the happy times before Gains's death, when Gregor and I had been friends and the warmth of his friendship had filled a gap in my life. There was more. Somewhere in the dim and feeble recesses of my mind, I had the idea that if I could get him to myself for an hour or two, I could solve the mystery of his recent behavior. It had something to do with the three pictures from Paris. I was sure of that. And I was sure I could find out. I really believed I was that clever. So when he mentioned staying to have dinner with him after we got to Long Island, I accepted that invitation, too.

The trip home on the Long Island Expressway was an education in all the things Lydia Wentworth had implied about Gregor's irresistibility. He went to work on me the minute Bennett left us, and he never let up. I'd been exposed to his charm before. It had been sweeping over me for years in waves. But they were nice, fatherly waves; beating out a father-daughter cadence I loved. This was different. I was being overrun—swamped—and deliberately.

It was a dazzling performance. Certainly it should have been an exhausting one for Gregor. In succession he was witty, attentive, cynical, frivolous, flattering, considerate, funny and brilliant. He was philosophical. He was deep. He was playful. He was everything a woman could want. I began to see, finally, what all those women saw in him that made him such a catch. My sides hurt from laughing at his stories. My face ached from smiling. My eyes felt soft as violets because he said they were. And I was doing my best to keep from being washed overboard, with only a one-finger clutch on the gunwales to keep me safe. Outwit Gregor? Fat chance! The day hadn't dawned when I could do that.

When we finally drove up to the house I was relieved, hoping that my bearings would be steadier once out of the isolation of the car. In a larger space I might be better able to function as an "immovable object."

"Cook's day off," Gregor said, opening the door. "Hope

you'll trust me not to poison you with my cooking. Come in."

He set about throwing together one of his famous omelettes while I addressed myself to a whiskey sour he'd made me. It was the first of several, and I should have known better.

After dinner he made stingers, and I was practically floating. I hadn't eaten since morning and it had been a long day.

From then on events become something of a blur, although certain recollections emerge in hazy vignettes. I'm afraid I remember singing a good deal, with Gregor struggling to support me on the piano. He had the gift of making everyone sound good. I thought I sounded divine, croaking away at "The Man That Got Away," "Paper Moon," and other vintage numbers. Gregor kept encouraging me by thinking of new songs and telling me I was marvelous. I remember talking mostly in French, a habit I often have after one drink too many.

Then we turned on the stereo and danced, and Gregor was a wonderful dancer. We used to say that if he ever lost all his money, he could make his living as a gigolo, and it was true.

"Vernon and Irene Castle!" Gregor shouted, and we did our own rather snappy version of the Castle Walk.

"Fred Astaire and Ginger Rogers!" This was a real challenge, and we went all out to meet it, whirling and leaping and stamping in colossal feats of athletic endeavor I wouldn't have dreamed we were capable of. Gregor was, of course, suitably debonair as he led me through intricate patterns, over chairs and tabletops. Then, in an excess of enthusiasm, I rushed outside and tried to do dance steps on the railing of the big, old veranda that ran around two sides of the house.

But the altitude must have sobered me somewhat because when Gregor followed me outside, still dancing, and said, "Fonteyn and Nureyev!" I demurred, finally.

"What are you trying to do, kill me?" I panted. There

was a fat, comfortable-looking chaise on the porch, and I made for it, thoroughly winded.

"I adore you, darling girl," Gregor told me, bending over and stroking my damp forehead. "And what you need is another drink."

Another drink was the last thing I needed, but I was in no condition to know it. Also, I had been very busy getting myself into the chaise, and now that I was in it, I didn't even want to make the effort to argue. I am a leaf that has drifted down to earth, I told myself. I have just landed, ever so softly. I will rest here, leaflike, forever and ever.

I closed my eyes. I may even have taken a short nap because it seemed like a long time before Gregor came back and sat down beside me and began to stroke my arm. He pressed a glass in my hand. "Absent friends."

"Can't . . . can't possibly."

"Lydia Wentworth, absent friend. Mustn't refuse to drink to her. Sacrilegious, like refusing to drink the Queen's health!"

I managed a sip, and Gregor was pleased. He seemed to be rewarding me with a kiss, or did I imagine it? My eyes were still closed.

"Let's call her up. Be fun," he suggested. I thought I could feel his moustache tickling me. Was it possible he was nuzzling my cheek? I considered opening my eyes to look, but it was too much trouble.

"Can't call. In Paris," I mumbled.

"Of course she is." Both his arms were definitely around me and squeezing. "But you know how to reach her. Miss Styles told you."

It would be very late in Paris, my befuddled brain tried to tell me. Who would dare to call her at such an hour? I wished he would go away so I could think better.

"Styles wouldn't tell," I managed. "Don't know." I screwed my eyes up tighter and tried to manage another little nap.

When I heard his voice again, it was just below my ear. I could even feel his breath, strong and warm. "Don't go to sleep on me, you silly thing. Wake up!"

Why is he talking to me in that tone of voice, I wondered. It doesn't sound very friendly. Does he think I can't hear him? Why, I was only catching a little wink, a tiny cat nap, that's all.

I opened my eyes with some difficulty and looked around for something to focus on. If I could concentrate on some object, my head would clear. It had always worked before. It was important to have a clear head. I was sure of that.

His breathing was awfully noisy. I could hear every breath going in and out like a bellows, and it alarmed me. How embarrassing if it were passion, after all these years! Maybe it was just too much to drink. People got strange ideas then. I must concentrate. I must cope. I repeated these sentences over and over until the words stopped making sense to me. So I made a supreme effort, staring through the window into the lighted inside of the house. The living room fell obediently into place, all its details clear after a second or two. I could see the empty dinner plates still on the table. Remembering that I had eaten, I felt better momentarily until my stomach flopped in an unwelcome confirmation of the meal.

The voice in my ear was complimenting me. "Good girl, Persis. Keep those eyes open. This is important, so listen. What did Gainsborough Brown tell you about his paintings before he died?" Gregor was shaking me—imagine! "He always told you everything, didn't he, Persis? Now tell me . . . tell me . . ."

Shaking me, for Heaven's sakes! I should have been indignant, but I was only mildly astonished. At this moment, in my mental disarray, I could only react to one thing at a time; and I was already deeply involved with mirrors and angles of reflection.

The opposite wall—let's see. There should be a mirror that would show that wall. If I twisted my head just a centimeter . . . It wasn't easy. My head felt like a half ton. But I managed it.

And suddenly there he was, reflected in the mirror.

Watching us. He could have been watching us for some time. Looking straight through the mirror at Gregor and me on the veranda. The man in the green car.

"Tell me, Persis. Tell me now," Gregor said.

I screamed. Just once, but it was good and loud.

Gregor let go of me as if I were a hot potato.

———

Mrs. Howard was waiting up for me when I got back to my house. Gregor had driven me home after making a cursory search for the intruder. He took the whole affair much too casually, I thought, and nothing would persuade him to call the police. He had hustled me out in a hurry, implying that I'd had too much to drink, and was silent during the ride.

She was sitting primly on one of the petit point chairs in the living room. She must have been sitting there for hours, her arthritic hands folded primly in her lap, her small and shapeless feet placed squarely side-by-side on the rug, her spectacles shining purposefully in the lamplight.

"I'm sleeping here nights from now on, Mrs. Willum," she announced, very determined. "You did your best to straighten this house, but you can't fool me. I haven't been taking care of it all these years for nothing. We got broke into last night, didn't we? I found the busted screen. So don't bother to tell me to go home. I'm staying. I already moved into the guest room and there I stay until you find out who done it."

I wanted to kiss her, I was so relieved, but she would have been furious. Then I wanted to cry, and that would have been just as bad. So I only said, "Thank you." I was still feeling pretty rocky.

She tactfully said good night and started up the stairs. Then she remembered something.

"Those questions you asked me ... I been thinking all day. You got an idea somebody's looking for something somebody else left here, right? Well, if you ask me, they're looking in the wrong place. But OK, I wrote down a list for you. It's on the table there. Good-night, now."

"Good-night, and bless you." I meant every word.

Then I settled down to read what she had written and wait for Susan Evans to arrive.

The list was there, as Mrs. Howard had said, propped up against a lamp where I would be sure to see it. It wasn't a long list, but I knew that if Mrs. Howard had been thinking about it all day, it would be thorough. Her arthritis might have slowed her down physically, but she was still as sharp as they came.

She had written:

"1. Hardrock built a new outside bin for rubbage." Translated from Howardese, this meant that the handyman, Blackstone, had constructed a new covered bin for the garbage pails. Nothing there.

"2. Those robbers from Dennison and Hoyle finally done something about the leak in the guest bathroom." Those robbers were the plumbers, of course.

"3. Hardrock painted the kitchen. Got the color wrong. But I guess you knew that." I did.

"4. Gainsberg Brown come snooping around looking for a place to store some of his junk for free. Said he was running out of room in his studio and you wouldn't mind. Said our space wouldn't do in the end. I told him beggars shouldn't be choosers. He didn't like that much." Gains had been leaving things at my house ever since I met him. It was part of his cheapness that he couldn't bear to spend a cent for warehouse or storage fees.

"5. Miss Ives come by while you was in Paris to see if Mr. Brown left anything here. Said he had a new studio to put it in now. I told her we still had junk from the time before last, some old pieces of lumber but nothing new. Showed her lumber. She said she'd have it picked up, but she didn't." I didn't blame her.

"6. Hardrock replaced missing bricks in walk without being told." This was indeed news.

"7. TV repair service come for color TV. Three weeks late." Naturally.

"8. You're not counting Mr. Olitsky, are you? He's been in and out, leaving books and papers and pictures like always." Was I counting Gregor? I didn't know.

And that was it. Not much. I settled down to wait for Susan Evans. It was nearly dawn in Paris, so I couldn't call Aunt Lydie; but I did get the overseas operator and tried to get her number. There wasn't any. Either it was unlisted or it was under another name or she hadn't a telephone.

To help me keep awake while I waited for Susan, I pulled out my sketchbook, attempting to recreate the face that had appeared in the mirror and had penetrated my alcoholic fog in such a startling way. I studied my drawing carefully. The features had the hard, tight look I remembered. One of Muss's men was all I could come up with. Maybe when he got my note saying I couldn't think of acting outside the gallery in the matter of the work Gainsborough completed before his death, maybe then he would call off his dogs. I had enough problems with Gregor getting me tight and third-degreeing me about Gainsborough's paintings and Aunt Lydie's whereabouts. If only my head would stop throbbing so I could think! Or if only Susan Evans would come so I could get to bed!

But she didn't come. It got to be twelve thirty . . . quarter to one . . . one o'clock . . . two. And then I must have fallen asleep in the chair because when I woke up again, I ached all over and my watch said four thirty in the morning.

12

Both my telephones were ringing and I was knee-deep in papers and correspondence when Gregor ushered Dickie de Pauw into my office the next day.

"Show him something pretty," Gregor ordered, grinning as if nothing had ever happened. "He wants to give it to Eleanore for a present, and we want her to be happy with it."

"Anniversary," Dickie shouted. "Usually forget it."

My first reaction was to tell Gregor to show him the pictures himself. He'd just decreed that we would finally reopen the gallery within three weeks, which meant that I didn't even have time to breathe, since all the details were my responsibility.

My second reaction was to suggest that the two of them take the day off and go out and buy an historic pile. It was the only gift she would appreciate, since restorations were her chief occupation, after Dickie-watching. All of us had been tapped to help rebuild endless ruins. It was time for another now that her latest was almost completed.

My final reaction was that I wasn't being very gracious. If the old boy really wanted to give his wife a picture, then I would supposedly have a better idea than Gregor of what a woman would like. Supposedly. Gregor had a very keen idea of what women liked, as I ought to know.

I ushered Dickie downstairs, where the pictures were

stored. Since we weren't officially open yet, the boy who usually carried the paintings in and out of storage for the client to study in the specially lighted downstairs room wasn't on hand. I would have to do the lugging and hauling myself, and I wasn't looking forward to it.

There was a bad moment when I paused to press the hidden switch that opened the downstairs door. The little button in the wall wasn't actually very secret, but it was Gregor's pet security measure. He firmly believed that no burglar would be smart enough to find it, although we all were sure anyone with half a brain could figure it out. I always had a nervous twinge when I pressed it with someone standing behind me, as Dickie was now.

"Just show me what you have lying around," Dickie howled as I settled him down. His face was more flushed than usual, an alcoholic's mottled red mask that covered him from the bridge of the nose to the base of his cheeks.

"Been a bad boy. Must placate the Old Girl. Never tried a painting before, but they seem to be the big thing today. Personally, I wouldn't give house room to anything but a good sporting print. But this is for her, what?" He launched into a long and windy dissertation about polo ponies and the shortcomings of The Game as it was played today. When it had gone on long enough for me to be convinced that he was never going to come up for air, I simply began the job of hauling out pictures for him to look at while he talked. The system suited Dickie. Each time I left the room, he raised his voice enough decibels for me to hear him clearly and just went on talking, nonstop.

The storage room was spooky in the half light. I'd never liked being alone there. It was too big and too full of lifeless sculptured forms. Today, Gainsborough's collection of figures disturbed me particularly. They were lined up along one wall in a crazy assortment of shapes and angles where I had to pass them on my way to and from the picture racks. I caught myself watching them surreptitiously from the corner of my eye. They gave me the creeps, an effect Gains, rest his black soul, had no doubt intended.

Meanwhile, Dickie never stopped, as I dug out everything I thought Eleanore could possibly be interested in. I must have brought out thirty or forty pictures without any luck, and finally I resorted to "no man's land," the section where we stored what we fondly—and to his face—called Gregor's Deadbeats—the paintings that he should have second thoughts about, that were too terrible to show. It was a last resort, but I was getting desperate. Nothing had pleased Dickie so far, and my arms were about to fall off.

None of us ever went near "no man's land" if we could help it. But this was different. Maybe one of the Deadbeats would discourage Dickie, who seemed determined to take up my entire day.

The first thing I saw was an unmarked packing case. It must have been specially built, otherwise there would have been some legend on it. I stared, bemused.

"How about a painting by that girl who was with me at the drowning?" Dickie's voice carried clearly. He made Gains's death sound like an occasion—The Drowning, engraved invitations and ushers. "Wasn't she an artist? Or was she an actress? Know who I mean? How do I get in touch with her?"

So that was what this was all about. He was trying to find Susan Evans! A present for Eleanore, my foot. She probably wasn't even having an anniversary!

"Wouldn't want my wife to know, of course." Every word was clear as a bell. "Terribly jealous, you know. Matter of fact, she may have followed me here. Absolutely sure I heard footsteps before. Nothing wrong with my ears, you know. Supersensitive. Never had to watch for a pony coming up behind, always heard 'em. Remarkable gift. You hear anything?"

I hadn't. How could I above the noise he was making? For that matter, how could he? Anyway, the staff was wandering around the downstairs halls, mainly because that's where the rest rooms were. I began to work at the open end of the case. I could see that there were three newly framed paintings with the framer's sticker neatly applied. I drew them out carefully. Three Gainsborough Browns. The right period. The right size. The ones Gregor had bought in Paris. And all three unsigned. I noticed that at once. I'm trained to notice things like that.

There wasn't much time, with Dickie droning on in the next room. But it was time enough. I had them fixed in my mind like photographs before I shoved them back in. When I got home at the end of the day, I would be able to take them out of my mind and examine them as carefully as if they were actually before me.

Unsigned—that was the puzzler. Gains conceivably might have sold them abroad to get quick money without having to pay Gregor's commission and without being found out. He might even have done it out of pique. All that I could understand. But he could have gotten much more for them with his signature. Much more.

Two days later Gregor suddenly took it into his head to change the switch in the storeroom. He'd had a dream, he said, that someone had penetrated his security and rifled the storage area; but in the same dream he had invented a new lock-up system, infinitely superior to the first, and it was to be installed immediately. That was Gregor for you! This time the secret switch was to be inserted in the side of a picture frame hanging near the downstairs door. We would press it while pretending to straighten the painting, the downstairs door would open, and no one would ever imagine how it was done. Absolutely foolproof, he insisted proudly. We were always straightening pictures, weren't we?

I thought immediately of Dickie's remark about being followed. Not that I believed it for a minute; but if Gregor was alarmed enough to start changing locks, there might be something to it. I decided to have a look around the storage area just in case. In case of what, I wasn't sure.

But I'm glad I did because when I went downstairs, I

could see at once that Gainsborough's people had been tampered with. Plaster heads and hands had been removed and replaced. Clothing had been disturbed. Macabre as it might seem, Gainsborough's people had been searched!

I set the figures back in order, taking my time. No place to hide anything here. Nothing. No room. If Gains cached away anything, it had to be somewhere else.

And he must have hidden something. His house had been searched. My house had been searched. Now this. It occurred to me to go see if the three unsigned Gainsboroughs were still there, and they were, which must have been a relief to Gregor.

A familiar hard knot began to form in my stomach and I reminded myself that it is the little things that break one down. You always rise to the big crises somehow!

It was that way now. I had survived the shock of Gainsborough's death. I had survived the realization he had been murdered. I had overcome the terrors of having my house searched. I had lived through being followed, had even accepted with some equanimity the fact that I might still be followed, as this most recent episode suggested.

But the search of Gainsborough's people almost unglued me. Probably it was the implications that did it. Gainsborough's death wasn't something that was over and done with.

I had to tell someone. The person I selected was Oliver.

I had been seeing more and more of Oliver Reynolds, sliding back into something like our old childhood relationship. I didn't stop to think about what it meant when I marched back to my office, called Oliver and asked him to pick me up and take me somewhere where we could talk. I only knew that I felt much better when we pulled into the parking lot at the deserted beach, facing the sea, and I told him everything. Well, not everything, but enough.

I told him I was sure Gainsborough had been murdered. I told him my house had been ransacked. I said I'd been followed and had seen the same man in Gregor's house. I said I thought I was still being followed. I described the three paintings I'd found. I even added that the Gainsborough Brown figure-people had looked odd to me today, as if someone had dismantled them to search their insides. And I finished with a description of Gregor's strange behavior.

I might have told him more if he hadn't interrupted me. Taking my hand gingerly in his bony one, as if the slightest pressure might alarm me further, he said, "You must calm yourself, Persis, you really must. One of the reasons I've always loved you is for your lively imagination, but don't let it get you all upset. It isn't good."

I didn't understand at once. "But those three paintings are absolutely genuine, and Gains normally would never have let them go without his signature. Something is terribly wrong, Oliver, and someone ought to know in case anything happens to me."

"Why should anything happen to you?" He was being indulgent. "No, no, I believe you. Of course I do. But he might have sold them without a signature for quick cash. Or maybe you missed it. You only had a second or two, and he always hid his signature in with the brush strokes."

I shook my head stubbornly. "I would have seen it."

I searched Oliver's face for reassurance. It was terribly important to me right now to have an ally. But the expression on his face wasn't awfully encouraging.

We didn't talk for a while. His eyes avoided mine. When he did speak again, he seemed to be choosing his words with some care.

"Persis, my dear, I'm sorrier than I can say about this." He still wasn't looking at me. His eyes were fixed on the seascape with such concentration that I could almost believe he was counting the waves. "Men like Gainsborough Brown and Gregor Olitsky . . . why are you so attracted to them?" I couldn't believe my ears. What was he saying? "Olitsky is no prize, I agree. But murder? Not his line. Now if he's made you promises and not kept them,

I wouldn't be surprised. All I can tell you is that you'll get over it in time."

He said more, a lot more; but I didn't listen. I was drowning in a feeling of the most awful shame. Why, he was sorry for me! He believed that I had made it all up because I was disappointed in love! Any second now he would suggest that I see a good doctor, one who specialized in affairs of the head.

A silver sports car with the top down roared up behind us and began to do sweeping, increasingly fast figure eights in the paved area that stretched along adjacent to the beach. I turned to watch, shading my face with my hand. Whatever else happened to me in my whole life, I was determined at that moment not to let Oliver see me cry.

"Are you sure there isn't more to it, Persis? Have you told me everything?"

"Everything." My voice was thick and I despised myself for it.

I hadn't told him everything and all the way home I was glad of it. Now that I thought about it, Oliver had been gone a very long time getting me a drink at Aunt Lydie's party. Certainly he had been away long enough to go down to the pool and back. . . .

13

It was, of all people, Sidney Muss who finally told me about Gregor.

I had driven to town to see him, reeled in like a reluctant fish by a long string of telephone calls and the irresistible lure of "something very important" to tell me. I rationalized that I'd been dying to see his house, anyway.

It was famous. Countless words had been written about it, even in such far-flung publications as *Apollo* and *Réalités*, where editors had buried it (and their astonishment) among articles on such subjects as the lacquering of furniture with "vernis Martin" and the rediscovering of Gallo-Roman villages.

As I jockeyed into the space Muss had saved for me by the simple expedient of having his chauffeur and car plug up a hole in front of his entrance, pedestrians on 72nd Street were stopping to stare at the twenty-foot sculpture rearing up in front of his building. Across one side of it the artist had splashed "To Sidney Muss" in white paint. As a nameplate, it was more than adequate. No one could doubt that a patron of the arts lived inside.

Several ornate gates and doors had to be negotiated before a tough-looking butler admitted me to a downstairs hall and stood aside, with patience born of experience, to allow me time to look around and gasp. And I did gasp. Nothing had prepared me for the actuality of seeing Sidney

Muss reproduced over and over again in plaster, bronze, terra-cotta, stone, mixed media, paint, papier-mâché, etc. . . . in every style and every material imaginable.

"The townhouse is devoted exclusively to portraits of Mr. Muss from his collection," the butler intoned, very bored. He'd obviously said it a million times before. "The rest of the collection is in his other houses around the world."

"How about the sculpture outside?" I asked, just to be wicked.

"An abstract portrait, madame." He'd said that a million times, too. "It's considered one of the most interesting portraits, but Mr. Muss wants it understood that he never rejects any of them."

I was aware of that—everyone was. When his first collection turned out to be fake, Muss had struck back by adding a modern studio to the top of this house and making it available to his favorite artists (only the living need apply) day and night with models included. Loft space being what it was in New York, there were plenty of takers, especially since all Muss asked in return was a portrait of himself and one painting a year. The rent was cheap at half the price, with all the publicity the portraits received.

The subject was seated upstairs beneath a very large portrait of himself seated in the same chair in the same room. The only difference between the two was that the man in the picture was twice the size of the original and that the original was grunting into a telephone. There were about thirty-five other Musses in the room, and I was deep in contemplation of one made out of automobile parts when the telephone conversation ended. "No more calls," I heard him say. "Have the car here in exactly half an hour."

I turned around and found him watching me. "I leave for Kennedy shortly, but we've plenty of time. Please sit down, Mrs. Willum."

The furniture, without exception, was cream and gilt

and overstuffed and underbred, the sort of thing I imagined one might find in a New Orleans house of pleasure. I picked a chair and sat down, trying to appear self-assured.

Muss wasted no time in getting down to business. Spreading his fingers firmly over the arms of his chair so that the sleeves of his jacket hiked up and I could see the big gold "M" cuff links in his shirt, he plunged ahead. "He came in here last spring looking like ... like ..." He struggled over the choice of word but was defeated.

"Gainsborough Brown?" It was an easy guess. No one else left everyone speechless.

"Yes." For the very first time I detected a glint of expression in those obsidian eyes, one that resembled astonishment. "I should be used to artists by now. They're crazy, most of them. Can't be judged by ordinary standards. Dirty fingernails, old clothes. But this one . . ." Words eluded him again as he dug his own perfectly manicured fingernails into the chair and shuffled his feet in their fancy shoes.

I let myself imagine the scene as it must have taken place. Gains would be all dressed for town. He would have taken pains, as always, to wear something that would make people stop and stare in a city that had grown accustomed to eccentricities of all kinds. Would he wear the black velvet with the fall of white lace (never too clean) at wrists and throat? Or would it be the fringed leather suit with the ropes of silver disks cascading down the front of the beaded brocade Mississippi gambler's vest and topped with a planter's white hat? Whatever the costume, he would have entered this room with a pirate's swagger and worked himself into a chair (probably the very one where I now sat) with the agility of a wild animal going to ground. And then? Then he would notice the portrait behind Muss's head; and regardless of which role he had adopted for the interview—humble genius or arrogant supertalent—he would let his eyes rest on it for an extra minute while his lip curved slowly into a smile of disdain, a smile that would send one unspoken but clearly heard word ringing around the room: "garbage." I'd seen that trick a hundred times. It never failed to demoralize.

Muss had found his tongue again. "He had a proposition and I listened, as I do to all business propositions. He would steal the plans for Olitsky's proposed overseas operation, and if I would beat Olitsky to the punch with a gallery chain of my own, he would let me handle his work exclusively. I was to give him a large advance, and he would give me a group of paintings as a token of good faith."

I gasped at the mention of paintings, but Muss was still talking. "He wanted a million-dollar advance; that's all. Only a million dollars." I couldn't tell whether the sum shocked him or not. He sat neatly in his chair as if he met a scoundrel like Gainsborough Brown every day of the year. I tried to reason it out. For the price of a few drinks Gains could probably get the plans from a befuddled Withers. Every cent Gregor had would be tied up in the new enterprise—nothing left over for more advances for Gainsborough. And, of course, Gains had neither loyalty nor scruples, only greed.

And paintings were cropping up again, paintings we had known nothing about. The same ones offered to Oliver?

"What did you do, Mr. Muss?"

"Well." He shifted slightly, but he wasn't squirming. "I had toyed with the idea of going into the gallery business. I have more paintings than I can use; half of them are in storage. On the other hand, I like being a collector." Naturally. A collector has more prestige.

I felt I couldn't stand it one more minute. "So . . ."

"So I refused. Anyway, what did I want with his paintings? They weren't even signed! If he'd signed them, I might have been tempted. But after my experience with fakes, you couldn't pay me to buy an unsigned painting. Artists can die . . ." He looked at me meaningfully. "Where would I have been then with my unsigned 'masterpieces'? With my history, would anyone have believed they were genuine? No. No deal like that for Sidney Muss."

"How many paintings did he offer, Mr. Muss?"

"I don't remember exactly, but it was more than a dozen."

More than a dozen! No wonder there was a search going on! Even without signatures those paintings, if they still existed, represented a monumental sum.

The butler had appeared and was whispering to Muss, who got up and said it was time for him to get ready to leave. "You can see the studio if you want to before you go as long as they're through working up there. Max, flick on the monitor and see if they're through. Most people like to see it."

I hadn't noticed the television monitor before, but now I saw the closed-circuit apparatus wedged under a painting that looked more like a picture of a lightning storm than of the collector. The butler stepped in front of the machine and bent over it, blocking the screen. Muss moved toward the door, saying to me as I followed, "By the way, Mrs. Willum, I hope you tore up that drawing the other night?" His tone was lightly tense.

I assured him that I had.

"Good." An impatient glance at the butler, who was still fiddling with the monitor. "Do something to it, Max. Tap it, that always works." Then he began to speak softly, as if what he was saying had no importance at all. "You might like to know that Olitsky came back on the same plane with you from Paris—only in economy. My men lost him after Customs. But he was here the night of July Fourth, all right."

"What?" He might just as well have walked up and punched me in the solar plexus.

"Didn't know that, did you? So don't waste fifteen thousand dollars' worth of loyalty on him, Mrs. Willum. Think it over. It's not too late to do business with me."

With that beautiful exit line he walked out of the room. I never doubted for a moment that Muss was telling me the truth. Don't ask me why.

Nor did I doubt for a moment that the dozen or so

paintings offered to Muss were the ones offered to Oliver, and that the three Gregor bought abroad were part of the same group, and that Gregor suspected there were more around when he quizzed me that night at his house. At least I now knew what the search was for.

The butler gave the television a disgusted thump. "Go on up. This thing's not working. All over the house there's always one that's not working. They should be nearly ready for a lunch break up there anyway. Take the elevator and stay as long as you want. Mr. Muss loves to show off his studio."

I thanked him and made my way over to the elevator. It whirred softly, taking me aloft. Then it stopped and I stepped out into the most beautiful studio I had ever seen. Two full stories high, and a painter's dream.

Obviously, no expense had been spared. The best architects and lighting engineers must have been retained because the whole place was filled with an approximation of the painter's favored north light, drenched everywhere. It was artificial but so cleverly installed that one wasn't aware of that. And equipment—it was all there, the best easels, sculpture stands, welding materials, setups, armatures, huge metal sinks, racks, shelves. Sidney Muss had done this studio in a big way, and done it well.

There were two people visible. One was an artist, enveloped in turpentine fumes, slashing away at a big canvas with the fury of a man engaged in a duel over an affair of honor. I knew him—Vic Longmaier, a nice guy who had turned a small gift for academic painting into a surprising success. I vaguely remembered that he was one of Muss's protégés and doing better every day. They loved his work in Texas, where the rich ranchers and oil men scrambled to get his latest things.

The other person was a model, sitting on the arm of an old white wicker chair with a spreading fan back. She was turned away from me, hair blazing in the light, the fiery halo of it adding lustre to the cream of her shoulders and back. She was fine-drawn and fragile, and she was utterly and beautifully naked.

I knew I couldn't stay. I would be intruding on her dreamy concentration and on his creative frenzy. Neither of them had even heard me enter.

I felt behind me for the button that would summon the elevator and was quietly waiting for it when a great crash of sound violated the stillness of the room. A furious voice, monstrously amplified, thundered from a speaker somewhere over my head. "Out!" it shouted. "Out of there! No visitors allowed while the artist is working! I told you that! Take that elevator straight down to the street and out, Mrs. Willum! It's a rule that's never broken. Out!" Muss's disembodied voice was strangled with rage. Hearing it now, I recognized it as the voice of one of the two angry men that night in the darkness of Aunt Lydie's party. Had the other man been Gainsborough Brown? "If you'd rather wreck your reputation than meet my price . . ." A threat of blackmail? And Muss, "Play games with me and you get hurt . . . " What had Gains had on him?

At the first sound through the speaker, the painter had jumped and knocked his canvas off the easel. The girl's head jerked around. I was pressing the elevator button so hard that I broke my fingernail.

It felt like an eternity before the doors slid open and gave me sanctuary, but it couldn't have been because Susan Evans's face was still frozen and the painter hadn't even made an attempt to pick up his canvas.

14

It took me just twenty-four hours after that frightening descent in the elevator to arrange a meeting with Susan Evans. The idea was forming even as the last of Muss's doors and iron gates closed behind me, and I flung myself into my little car and drove away. Muss had scared me good and plenty but not so much that I couldn't think.

The minute I recognized Vic Longmaier as the artist who was painting her, I knew I could figure out a rendezvous. Marvin Greenspan was Vic Longmaier's dealer, and his gallery was just around the corner from Muss on Madison Avenue. Greenspan was a friend of mine. To be accurate, he was a friend of everyone and everyone was a friend of his. He was really a collector who had backed into the business without realizing it.

He wasn't even at his gallery full time. In the mornings he helped his four uncles run a private hospital on the South Shore of Long Island. Greenspan's artists didn't begrudge the time he spent there. They never knew when they themselves might need the facilities. The hospital always had half a ward full of sick artists or their needy dependents.

When I reached Marvin on the phone, he couldn't have been nicer. "You want to talk to that girl in private? No problem. I'll fix it for you. Couldn't be easier. I'll work out an airtight little plot. Be here at noon."

So it was arranged.

When she walked into Greenspan's tiny office where I was waiting, it was as if someone had turned on a searchlight, for the whole room lit up. It wasn't just her blaze of hair—she had tied a long, chiffon scarf around her head and most of her hair was hidden. It was her special aura—that willowy body and the face like a Burne-Jones.

"Mr. Muss must have turned on one of the other monitors in the house. He has them all over," she said. "You see, he doesn't want any of his social friends to know about me. He has Max keep watch on me when he's away."

"How did you get out of there today?"

"Mr. Greenspan called up and said one of Vic's clients was in town from Cleveland and wanted to talk to Vic about a commission. Since everything would depend on having the right model, the client could look me over after lunch. Mr. Muss wouldn't object to that." She didn't act as if she believed it. She had closed the door behind her and was pressing herself against it.

"Why didn't you come to my house that night?"

"You don't understand about Mr. Muss, but then, how could you?" She sat down finally, after first moving her chair around to face the door. Her feet were well under her, and she was poised for flight. "I want to thank you for not telling him you saw me on the street with Gainsborough Brown. I remember you staring at us out of that elegant car. I wasn't supposed to know Gains . . ." She paused.

For a moment her fear was contagious, and I found myself glancing at the door, too. So I reassured her, "I haven't told anyone. But I think you owe me an explanation."

She nodded but didn't speak at once.

"Were you with Sidney Muss the night he came to my house?" I asked.

"Yes. He sometimes takes me with him at night, but only at night, and I'm never allowed out of the car." Her eyes were busily examining the room—the tiny bathroom, its door ajar, the Raoul Dufy painting resting on a velvet chair that had a spotlight attached to its back, the Camoin watercolor on the wall behind my head, the pictures stacked against the wall back to back and face to face, the tempestuous Vlaminck on the far wall.

There was nothing there to frighten her. Nevertheless (or maybe because of it), she began to cry. Tears spilled over and ran down her face, taking her eye makeup with them. She made no effort to dry them. It was as if she had no feeling in her face at all.

"If I hadn't helped Gainsborough . . . I must have been crazy . . . and that figure we made . . ." The beautiful aquamarine eyes were fixed on some unpleasant vision.

"Figure?"

"*The Collector*—the figure sitting on the beer cans—the fat one, holding the house. That's Mr. Muss. He's never seen it, but he knows something like it exists and he has to have it."

"Perhaps you'd better tell me," I suggested softly.

And she did, starting each time the little bell under the mat in the gallery entrance buzzed to signal someone's arrival. Her voice rose, faded and sometimes stopped altogether, and her eyes never ceased their nervous wandering, but she talked.

She was an actress out of work most of the time and just managing to get along by posing for artists and doing once-in-a-blue-moon walk-ons in television soap operas. It was a hard life, and she was pretty much at the end of her rope when Muss's men stopped her on the street one day and asked her if she'd be interested in well-paid work. She was suspicious until she found out who her employer was to be. Muss was a big name, and she was thrilled. He explained to her when she went to see him that it was strictly a business proposition. He would pay her not to accept any other jobs but just to be available to him any time he wanted to see her. Absolutely no sex would be involved; it was just that he liked to surround himself with beautiful things and was willing to pay for the privilege.

"It was a kind of proposition I wasn't used to. And the money was good, so I jumped at it."

I was astonished. This smashing, long-legged girl . . . how could she have been so naive? "You believed him?"

She looked full at me, eyes wide. "Of course. I wanted to. He was so rich. I had all sorts of wild dreams about his marrying me. That was at first."

She must finally have tasted the tears on her lips because she had found a handkerchief and was dabbing at her cheeks.

"I had to be around day and night. His men would call for me at all hours. Sometimes I'd just hang around. Sometimes I'd pose for the artists in his studio. Mr. Muss was right about one thing," she continued, her voice very low. "There wasn't any sex. I think it was worse because he was always watching. He'd never touch me, but those eyes . . . watching, watching, watching. He had a thing about touching flesh. He just wanted to see, even when I was in the studio." She rose unsteadily and began to search the shelves behind Greenspan's desk. "Do you suppose he has a bottle here somewhere? They always do. I really could use a drink."

But there wasn't any. Nothing in the bathroom, either.

"I don't believe Greenspan drinks," I told her.

She sighed and forced herself to sit down and continue.

"It was sick, Mrs. Willum. It began to make my flesh creep. He was *so* weird that he began to make me weird. I got so I couldn't sleep, afraid they'd call. I began to take baths all the time, scrubbing my skin until it hurt. Once I cut up all my clothes with a scissors and had to call a friend to bring me more. I reached a point where I felt if I didn't see people my own age—normal people—I would kill myself."

She got up and went into the bathroom; she was going to settle for a drink of water.

"One night when Mr. Muss was out of town, I filled myself with drinks and false courage and went out to an artist's party. I was sure Mr. Muss's men watched my every move while he was away, but I didn't care. I was desperate. I borrowed a black wig from a friend, put on dark glasses and just went. Gainsborough Brown was there."

So that was how she'd met him.

"I'd become sort of an art buff by now because of posing for so many artists. It rubs off on you. And I was thrilled to meet Gains. I'd even collected some of his posters once. As a matter of fact, the posters started it all."

I was paying strict attention.

"I had all the posters except the one from his first show. They're impossible to find. So when I met him, I came right out and asked if he had any and could I buy one from him. I don't know how I ever got up the nerve. Well, he was flattered and took me off to his studio right then. That was his old studio."

"West Eighty-sixth Street," I said.

"I guess so. It was when his studio was still in town. We had some more drinks and made love not too efficiently. Then he started poking around in those great big drawers, looking for my poster and cursing his secretary beneath his breath. I remember that because I was surprised he had a secretary. Most artists can't afford one. Finally he gave up looking in the drawers and took one of the framed ones off the wall and started to take it apart."

Typical, I thought, seeing the scene vividly in my mind's eye. He'd give her the poster because it didn't cost him anything, but he'd be too cheap to give her the frame. Even sex didn't interfere with Gains's parsimony. "Then what?"

"He seemed to be having trouble. There were other things stuck in behind. They looked to me like unstretched canvases, but I only got a quick glimpse. I don't think he expected to find them there because he got this funny look on his face and put everything down and told me to get out, just like that. I had to get home as best I could."

Every instinct told me that this was a key part of the puzzle, this business about the posters. If only I could figure it out.

"He called to apologize the next day, and I began seeing him whenever and however I could. I shouldn't have, especially after he got married, but I just couldn't help myself. It was better than going mad. Oh, I tried to stop after he came back with a new wife. But as soon as he'd call I'd go running back to him, trying to think of new ways to hang on to him. That's how I began to make the figures for his last show."

"What?"

"That's right. He couldn't think of anything. He'd run dry. And as I say, I'd picked up a lot of ideas and some facility from all the artists I'd posed for. So I had this idea for the figures and he liked it. I made them in my apartment and he did the props, and it kept him coming to see me."

"Didn't Muss ever find out?" The very idea gave me goose bumps.

"He found out." She turned away, her whole body shrinking within itself for protection as she remembered. "One night they were waiting for me when I came back, and they took me to Mr. Muss. 'Don't really damage her,' he told them, 'not this time.' Then he sat and watched while two of them held me and the other one beat me. 'Don't bring her to me until I can look at her again,' he said. 'I only like beautiful things around me.' It was quite a while." She crossed her arms and held herself tightly, the way one cradles a child, and rocked gently back and forth.

Finally she roused herself. "He shouldn't have done that. He never gave me credit for being different from the other things in his collection. I had eyes and ears. And I'd found out a few things. Gainsborough gave me the idea of what to do and how to do it. He showed me how I could hurt Mr. Muss."

Blackmail. In my imagination, I saw Gains's wooden box with all the clippings about Sidney Muss. Gains must have had blackmail in mind from the moment Muss refused to go into business with him and give him a million-dollar advance. He must have stalked this girl from the minute he

112

learned she belonged to the collector, pumping her for information and placing her in jeopardy without hesitation.

"So we made *The Collector* because I found out that long before he became 'legitimate,' Mr. Muss was illegally in the beer-distributing business. And even worse, he ran a string of places, mostly down south, where a man could go and meet a girl and . . . And Mr. Muss used to watch them, too; there were peepholes. He's changed his appearance since then—he used to be big and fat. But he lives in dread that someone from his past might come along. So when Gains told him there was something in the new collection that would ruin him, he went bananas. Gains couldn't resist continuously upping the price; they were still bargaining when he died."

The buzzer on Greenspan's desk sounded and the voice of the girl who minded the gallery for him came over the intercom. "Mr. Greenspan and Mr. Longmaier and the other gentleman are crossing the street now, Mrs. Willum."

"Good. Have you noticed anyone who might be watching the gallery?" Of course, somebody from Muss would have followed her to make sure the appointment was on the level.

"There's been one man hanging around."

I spoke as firmly as I dared to the girl across from me. "Fix your face, Susan. You're going to have to go out there in a minute and talk to Vic and Marvin and the client so the story will be believable. Just tell me first, what were you doing at my aunt's party? Wasn't that dangerous?"

She laughed for the first time. "Life is a black comedy, only funnier, Mrs. Willum. Would you believe that a week after Gains had all the figures moved out of my apartment and into his own on Long Island, Mr. Muss *ordered* me to start seeing Gainsborough? Get next to him, he told me. Find out what's in his studio and report. Stick to him like glue. Isn't that hysterical? Naturally, I never told him what he wanted to know."

Her face was perfect now, eyeliner restored. The bell

under the front mat sounded three times in rapid succession. There was a spatter of conversation from the outer room, then Marvin Greenspan called, "Miss Evans, could you step out here, please?"

I nodded to Susan and she stood up, tugging her thin T-shirt down over her French denims, and stepped out into the gallery to be looked over by the "Cleveland client."

A few minutes later Marvin Greenspan poked his head around the door frame. He had snapping blue eyes and sideburns that threatened to overrun his whole face. It was the sideburns that had made me ask him to help today—they seemed to indicate that the fire of adventure still burned fiercely inside that rotund body.

"OK, they're all gone—Vic, the girl and the goon that was hanging around outside. Come out and meet a good actor and a good friend, and thank him for filling in."

He beckoned me out to the main gallery, and there was—Oliver.

"Meet the Cleveland buyer." Greenspan's eyes shone with mischief.

"Oh, no!" Oliver was the last, but *the* last, person I wanted or expected to see here. Or anywhere, after our little chat.

Oliver looked as startled as I did. "I didn't know you were mixed up in this, Persis."

I tried to look innocent.

"I recognized that girl. She's the one who found Gains in the pool, isn't she? What's going on?" His mouth was smiling, but his eyes weren't.

Greenspan saved me. "A girl wants a favor, you have to ask why? Isn't that her business? You got something against doing a nice lady a favor, Mr. Oliver Reynolds?" I could almost hear clanking as he buckled on his armor. "You heard what Vic Longmaier said at lunch. Muss keeps this beautiful redhead practically under lock and key. So who can speak to her if they want to? No one, that's who. Muss pretends it's because she drinks. So for drinking you keep a person locked up like an animal?"

Marvin Greenspan was completely aroused. He had enjoyed doing me a favor. His sympathies were thoroughly engaged by Susan. He had done a good deed, and no one was going to spoil it for him.

"This lady wants to exchange a few innocent words with somebody nobody ever gets to see. That's a game, you think? Listen, Mr. Former Art Critic, the next time you want a favor—like I should track down some special paintings for one of your films—you just ask me and see what happens!"

I began backing toward the door, Greenspan's comfortable bulk covering my retreat. This was a good time to go, while the little round man was still holding the bridge. If I stayed, Oliver would be asking more questions, and I never wanted to talk to him again.

15

It was a few days later that I was asked to keep my promise to Alida Brown's housekeeper, Maggie. Amid pledges of undying gratitude and floods of instructions on what to feed Alida, which pills to mete out to her and what keys to use to lock the doors, Maggie finally departed to spend a day and a night with her sister. That was all the respite Alida would permit her long-suffering housekeeper.

The poor woman was so excited at the prospect of a few hours of freedom that she jammed her navy blue straw hat all the way down to the tops of her ears when she said good-bye to me at the door. "I can't ever thank you enough, Mrs. Willum. If you ever want anything from me, just ask, please. My sister says the same. Her daughter will be home this weekend, and we're going to baptize the youngest grandchild. They've been waiting all this time to do it until I could come. Oh, thank you, ma'am." I had the impression that they were all afraid the child would die and be condemned to limbo before Maggie was released to attend the ceremonies.

Alida was downstairs today, stretched out comfortably on one of the faded gold brocade sofas in the barnlike drawing room. I'd been to see her several times since my first visit, and each visit had been more or less a repetition of the first—the shadow-filled bedroom . . . Alida on her bed of elegant linens . . . medications being brought in with the regularity of trains entering a station, not that I ever saw her actually take them. Finding her downstairs was encouraging. Maybe she was getting better.

I remembered the drawing room only vaguely from the night of Gains's death, when Oliver and I had brought Alida home. There had been other things on my mind then.

Now, in the light of day, the room revealed itself as yet another theme in the counterpoint of the entire house—decayed gentility and musty, deteriorated splendor. It was a big room, so big that voices chased fleeing echoes around the walls. It had furniture that must have been created to be lounged in by giants, since the legs and thighs of no ordinary mortal could ever settle comfortably in the depths of its seats and the far reaches of its backs. There was a fireplace with an opening big enough to accommodate a small cocktail party, exquisitely beautiful rugs on which a million moths had feasted and probably died of sheer bliss.

And in the midst of all this was Alida, lying on a barge-like sofa and looking like the Lily Maid of Gull Harbor, the Beauty to Gainsborough's Beast.

"I've determined absolutely that I will get better," she announced to me as I walked in. "I have decided that I must get well and see people and do things. I can't bring him back, so I must go on."

She didn't look any better to me. Just getting those few words out was an effort that left her panting. But I admired both her logic and her spirit, and I told her so. "Would you mind, Alida, if I did a portrait of you while I'm here? It will simply be a watercolor sketch, nothing formal. You needn't move. I'll do you just as you are." I'd brought my paints out with me, knowing that this would help us both to pass the time.

She was pleased with the idea, and we settled down to what promised to be an agreeable afternoon, with Alida talking in fits and starts but mostly drowsing, and me working away and chattering about anything I thought might divert her in the intervals when she appeared to be totally awake.

117

The afternoon passed quickly, and I was surprised when I noticed that the daylight was fading. I'd been too absorbed to notice the time—it's that way when you're painting—and furthermore, although by now I felt that I was totally familiar with the bones and textures and planes that comprised Alida's face, none of my sketches pleased me. I kept tearing them up and starting again, determined to capture the elusive quality that I perceived in her.

The clock in the hall was striking exactly five o'clock when Gregor pounded on the front door. The noise might have frightened us if we hadn't clearly heard his voice calling, "Let me in, ladies! One thirsty art dealer in desperate need of liquid refreshment after a hard day in the market!"

Alida had been half asleep. She awoke with a smile of delight. "Let him in, Persis. The new leaf . . . I start now."

I thought of the plane that had carried both Gregor and me back from Paris. "About Gregor," I began, "I'm not sure you should trust him. He . . ."

But Alida had made up her mind. "I know, Gainsborough said he was *méchant,* a rascal, wicked. I know all that. But he's fun . . . amusing. He will make me laugh. Let him in, Persis. Please."

So I did. Anyway, it seemed impossible that Gregor, with his Adolphe Menjou moustache and disarming smile, could be truly wicked. But what did wickedness look like, anyway? Ask me to draw a picture of evil and I wouldn't know where to begin—with a forked tail, perhaps, and Gregor wasn't wearing one of those.

"Hello, Gregor. How are you?" I opened the front door for him.

"Thirsty, as usual. Factory practically ground to a standstill without you today. Have a million things to discuss with you. Notes in my pocket. Had Withers write it all down." His quick eyes darted toward the drawing room. "Where's the beautiful Alida?"

"In here, Gregor." The sound came faintly from around the corner.

Gregor went toward it, moving, as he always did, on uncoiling springs. "You're downstairs, Alida. Great day! A celebration is called for."

Alida said she thought there might be a bottle of sherry in the kitchen, so I went off to fetch it. When I came back, balancing the offerings in three juice glasses on Alida's breakfast tray (there had to be wine glasses somewhere, but I didn't want to leave the two of them alone for the time it would take me to search the battery of cupboards), Gregor was entertaining Alida with some story about Dickie de Pauw.

"The old lecher has this thing for young girls, you know. So you can imagine how taken in I was by his needing a secretary to help him with his memoirs. . . ."

For an awful moment I thought that Dickie had approached Gregor in his search for Susan Evans, and I was afraid the association would be too painful for Alida. But I needn't have worried. Gregor was saying that Dickie had tried to hire away one of the young, part-time girls from the gallery. Good old Dickie, at it again!

"So I told him, look here, de Pauw . . ." I handed Gregor his glass of sherry and after taking a gulp he went on with his story, complete with a good imitation of the de Pauw wheeze-and-roar delivery. Alida was watching him closely.

Neither of them noticed that I had almost spilled my drink. Maybe it was the reiteration of the name de Pauw or the mention of his passion for girls. Perhaps it was my sudden, desperate alarm that Gregor would bring up the woman so closely associated with Alida's bereavement. I'm such a hopelessly visual person . . . and suddenly there she was, conjured up full-form in my mind: I could see Susan Evans surrounded by admirers, a little the worse for champagne, but still charming and just a bit reckless, taking off her long cloak so she could display her costume, reaching back without looking to throw it over a chair or simply dropping it on the ground with a careless gesture. And in my vision, while Susan was in the midst of her

119

innocent showing off, a hand reached out, unnoticed, picked up the cloak and drew it back into the shadows. Later it would certainly serve as the perfect cover for anyone who might be seen walking with Gainsborough Brown. No one would have noticed the sleight of hand. They all would have been watching the strikingly lovely Susan Evans disrobe.

Except ... there might be one person, just one, who would have seen.

I came out of my reverie with a start and glanced at Gregor and Alida. No need to worry about them. He was talking to her nonstop, making full use of the first real opportunity he'd had to cast his spell upon her. There was a touch of color in her cheeks. She was enjoying it.

"I think I'll have a look in the kitchen while you're keeping Alida company, Gregor. I want to see what Maggie left for me to fix for dinner."

They barely looked at me. They wouldn't even know I was gone until Gregor ran out of steam, and that wouldn't be for some time. I had noticed that one of the house telephones was in the kitchen; Alida and Gregor couldn't overhear even if they paused long enough to miss me.

I left the room, making myself walk slowly as if I had nothing on my mind, afraid that my rising sense of excitement might somehow communicate itself to them. But once in the cavernous kitchen I moved swiftly, dialing the telephone number with fingers that shook with urgency.

"Mrs. de Pauw, please," I said to the answering voice. Dickie's wife was a woman who watched her husband's every move. Years of monitoring the activities of an antique Don Juan would have taught her never to miss a trick. If she had noticed—if only she had! I screwed my eyes tight and prayed as hard as I ever had in my life while the person on the other end of the connection went off to find Eleanore. It took forever. I had run out of prayers and was simply crossing my fingers by the time the person came back to report that Mrs. de Pauw had just driven away.

They couldn't stop her in time. Off to cocktails somewhere. Wouldn't be back until eight thirty or so. Was there a message?

I thought wildly. By the time Eleanore returned, I would be alone with Alida. It wouldn't do for her to know I suspected Gainsborough had been murdered. She was in enough of a state as it was. I couldn't call back tonight. On the other hand, if Eleanore could begin to try to remember . . .

Yes, there was a message, I said. Could the person write it down? It was fairly long, I was sorry to say. They could? Good! I was Mrs. Willum, and I was drawing a series of vignettes from Miss Wentworth's birthday party. Wentworth, that's right. And I wondered if Mrs. de Pauw could remember who picked up the cloak the model Susan Evans had dropped on the ground so I could include that person in the picture. Did they have the message?

They did. The person read it back to me verbatim, and we hung up. I shouldn't have done it that way. I should have waited, keeping my inclination to act on the spur of the moment, for once, firmly in hand. But my need to know lent itself to impulsiveness. My visual hunch seemed to have a will of its own, demanding verification.

I quietly replaced the receiver and heaved the great sigh that comes with a deed well accomplished. Then I heard the whoosh of the pantry door swinging shut and saw a face looking at me through the serving window into the kitchen.

"I came out to refill the, ugh, sherry." Gregor's fine white teeth were bared in what would have passed anywhere in the world for a friendly smile. "I'd forgotten what an awful drink it is. Although I admit it's great for cooking, and I once kept an elderly dog alive on it for over a year."

He couldn't have heard anything. Not through the thick pantry door, I reassured myself.

I found the sherry and poured it into his glass without spilling a drop.

After dinner Alida grew visibly nervous. Gregor had long since gone, leaving me with a long list of gallery instructions, which gave fair warning that with the opening of the season imminent, I could not spare many more hours away from my desk.

There had been a few nervous moments when he brought up the subject of Gainsborough's birthday present to Aunt Lydie—the sculpture that had never been unveiled. He wanted to borrow it for a one-night exhibition at the North Shore Gallery as a preseason opening, and he requested that I ask my aunt's permission to exhibit it. "She'll be less likely to say no to you, Persis. Tell her I'm building an outdoor art show around it—proceeds to benefit the Gainsborough Brown Art Scholarship. She shouldn't turn down such a worthy cause." I was afraid Alida might be upset by the reminder of Gainsborough, but she didn't seem to be and even offered to appear at the gala if she was up to it.

When he was gone, I handed Alida her pills and applied myself to fixing a dinner that would appeal to an invalid's appetite. I must say, the tray I brought in looked inviting (I am a reasonably good cook when I put my mind to it); but although Alida made a polite show of enjoying it, all she really did was to rearrange the mounds of the food on her plate, making indentations with her fork.

Afterward I suggested a game of gin rummy, and she made a half-hearted attempt at playing, but her mind wasn't on the cards. Her sole conversational overture consisted of mentioning how amusing Gregor was and wondering why I didn't trust him. She herself seemed nervous about Miss Ives, but I couldn't make such sense of it; and as the hours passed, she became more and more preoccupied and fretful, glancing out the windows at the deepening shadows and looking toward the hallway like a person anxious to be safely upstairs for the night. Finally she put down her cards and said, "It's dark now, Persis, and I'm terribly tired from being downstairs all day. Would you mind if we went to bed? First, you must check all the windows and lock them. And did Maggie explain about the doors? Hadn't you better start to inspect everything now?"

I told her I would. Then she didn't want to be left alone and insisted on accompanying me through the mammoth house while I tested every latch and turned the key in every door. When we were done, she was whimpering with fatigue. "I'm so tired. I think I will have to go right up this minute. Yet, I hate to. To tell you the truth, Persis, I've been in that room so long that sometimes I feel like an animal in a cage. And yet I'm so tired, so very tired."

"Why sleep there if you hate it so? Has it ever occurred to you that part of the problem might be simply that the room holds memories of you and Gains?" I didn't want to go on. I might just upset her more.

But she seemed interested. "I had never thought of that. But of course! When I'm in that room, I'm depressed and all I think about is him and what happened. That room is full of him. And I keep going over and over in my mind the uselessness of the accident and wondering why it had to happen. Why Gains?"

"Well, there you are. Why not take my bed? Try it. See if it helps. If it doesn't, we can change back again."

"Would you mind? We'd be right across the hall from each other. Maybe it would work. My bed was made up fresh this morning."

I had a notion I wouldn't sleep too well in her bed, either. Her room depressed me, just as this entire house depressed me. But my sleep didn't matter for one night; hers did. "Of course, I don't mind," I fibbed. "Just hop into bed, and I'll bring my things across the hall to your room. I may read for a while if it won't bother you."

I found her medicines and her nightgown, and gathered them up for her. Although it wasn't yet nine o'clock, she was so tired that I didn't think she needed the sleeping pills Maggie had ordained; but I left them on the table next to her bed just in case. When I said good-night, she had already snuggled deep under the covers with her eyes closed. I left both our doors open so that I'd be sure to hear her if she woke during the night. I was sure she wouldn't.The change of scene already seemed to have done her good. She hadn't cast one worried glance at the windows opening onto the balcony and outside steps that exactly matched those of her own bedroom. Anyway, the French doors were secured; I'd tested them.

I found a Regency romance in her bedroom and settled down with every intention of reading until I couldn't keep my eyes open, but then I realized that the light from the reading lamp must be streaming across the hall directly into Alida's eyes. I switched it off and tried to sleep, but it was hopeless. The room was unbearably stuffy with the French doors closed so I got out of bed very quietly, knowing Alida would have a fit if she heard me, and fumbled around in the dark trying to open them. After a minor struggle with the latch, I succeeded. Cool air flooded into the room, and I stood savoring it for a minute or two, taking welcome breaths of it. The balcony looked inviting, but I didn't dare to step outside. Alida might hear me.

Instead, I drew the curtains back and left the French doors wide open to the night breeze. It was very still except for the friendly chorusing of the tree toads and an occasional rustle of leaves. After a last wistful look, I went to bed and finally fell asleep.

I couldn't have been sleeping long when something woke me. I forgot where I was. Then I realized that Alida was standing over me and whispering, "Persis. Persis. Please wake up. Wake up." I could just make out her form in the dark.

I flailed my way up through the layers of sleep. "What is it?" I struggled to focus my attention.

"Are you all right? It took so long for you to answer."

"What's wrong?" I made a move to turn on the light. I was alert now.

"No, no, don't." She was still whispering. "Didn't you hear the noise? It sounded outside this room. I was afraid. Don't turn on the lights. I have a flashlight."

124

"I didn't hear anything." But could I trust myself? I had been more exhausted than I had expected and had been sleeping soundly. I listened carefully, noting that a real wind had come up and was now lashing through the trees. The stars had disappeared. "It must be the wind. Hear it? Maybe a plant fell off the balcony. Or a dead limb came down somewhere. Shall I look?" I reached for the flashlight, but she drew back.

"How silly of me! I never thought of that. No, don't bother. I'm sorry I woke you. It's just that I'm so jumpy all the time! The wind. Of course. I'll go back and take my pill and not bother you again. Yes, I hear the wind now." She started to turn away, then hesitated. "But I'll leave the flashlight here in case you need it."

I took it from her. "All right, Alida, don't you worry. Go on back to bed. As you can see, everything's really perfectly all right."

"I'm going. Sorry I disturbed you, Persis."

"Good-night."

After that I fell into a state of half sleep, half listening. I don't know how long I'd drifted along that way when I actually did hear a crash. It was good and loud, and it sounded like something smashing onto the bricks directly under the balcony. I was out of bed in an instant, on my feet with the flashlight ready in my hand and every nerve in my body vibrating. Suddenly the slightest night sound seemed ominous.

I moved toward the open doors, at the same instant switching on the flashlight and swinging the arc of light back and forth as widely as I could. Nothing there. I stood in the door and illuminated the balcony and the steps leading down the side to the double-level terrace far below. Still nothing. Finally, I stepped bravely out onto the balcony itself and leaned toward the railing so I could shine my light directly onto the edges of the terrace and the spreading lawns.

A gust of wind saved my life. By purest chance, at the very moment I put my hand on the railing, it blew across my face, whipping my nightgown into one of the espaliered rose trees that stood in wooden tubs along the balcony. My reaction was sheer instinct. I pulled back to save my gown from the thorns; and as I did, the entire section of railing went over the side with a crash. I would have gone with it had I not changed my point of balance just in time.

For a long time I pressed myself against the side of the house, trying to melt into it, afraid to move. I couldn't control the tremors that racked me. It seemed they would never stop, and I remember thinking that this must be what people meant when they talked about shaking like a leaf. Only it was more like a whole forest of trees. I must have turned off my flashlight because when I finally moved back into the house—I have no idea how long it was—I had to feel my way like a blind person.

Somehow I locked the French doors. Somehow I got myself back into bed. And somehow, just as the first misguided bird woke up and gave voice in the still blackness, I fell into a restless semi-sleep.

All this time there had been no sound from Alida. She must have taken her sleeping pill.

When it was really light, I got out of bed and made myself return to the balcony to try to establish what had happened. How harmless it looked in the daylight! Even the railing looked innocent—an honest piece of workmanship that had given years of good service, now rotted with age. It was careless but not sinister that no one had noticed, no one had repaired it. So the merest pressure of my hand had dislodged a section. Whom could I blame?

I even found a broken flower pot, smashed to bits in the middle of the teardrop-shaped bricks of the lowest level of the terrace, and I wondered if it had truly been the wind . . . or someone trying to get into Alida's room last night. I kept thinking about it as I picked up the scattered pieces and hid them in the shrubbery. I wasn't going to frighten Alida by telling her.

But I had to mention the railing. "You ought to have this repaired as soon as you can," I told her later on, pointing out the gap in the railing. "That must have been what you heard last night. It would make quite a crash."

But she wasn't deceived. "Oh, Persis," she cried, clutching her wrapper. "I was right. Someone wants to kill me. I was supposed to be in that bedroom last night!"

16

Every now and again one hears the remark that in this day of jet travel, it is possible to dine in Paris one night and be back in New York for dinner the next; but I wouldn't want to try it. As it was, I was about to try something almost as exhausting: a flight that would give me two full days in Paris and get me home by the following mid-afternoon.

I pretended to myself that it was a spur-of-the-moment decision, brought on by the near-catastrophe on Alida Brown's balcony. She definitely needed help, and a trip to France might be part of the solution.

But was it really so unplanned? Or was I really running to that enigmatic, all-powerful figure, Aunt Lydie, just as I had always done whenever things began to close in on me? Was I rushing to Paris because there was no other way to talk to her, since I'd learned days ago that no telephone was listed for her at the address I'd found in her office? Why else had I been carrying my Air Travel card in my handbag along with all the other credit paraphernalia that make moving around the world so simple? I even had my passport with me, up to date and tucked into a compartment of my handbag.

The minute Maggie appeared at Alida's house, I threw my little overnight case into the car and drove directly to Kennedy. A first-class ticket was no problem—it never was. And there was plenty of time before the nine-thirty departure to telephone my house. The terminal was comparatively empty at this hour of the morning. Most of my fellow passengers were men who looked like transoceanic commuters, bored by the prospect of yet another session with cramped knees and dull movies. I saw no sign that I was being followed, although I couldn't be certain.

Mrs. Howard answered on the fifth ring. "Yes?" She sounded cranky at being interrupted at her chores.

"I'm going to be out of town for a couple of days, Mrs. Howard, and I want you to do a few things for me."

"Sure. What do you want me to do?"

"First, tell anyone who calls that I'm in bed with the flu and not to be disturbed. Tell them I'm taking a million pills but that I feel too rotten for visitors or anything. I don't care how you do it—just keep pretending I'm there but mustn't be disturbed."

"Right. The flu's all over the place." Mrs. Howard loved intrigue almost as much as she loved other people's illnesses. She'd manage, embellishing reports on my condition with lurid medical details. "What else?"

"If Mrs. de Pauw hasn't called by the end of today, telephone her tomorrow and ask her if she got my message. If she did and has an answer, make a note of what she says and don't lose it."

"OK. Mrs. de Pauw. Got it. Anything else?"

There was. I'd been trying to escape it ever since Alida stepped out on her balcony this morning. It was the complete fatalism expressed on her face when she saw the broken railing, and the way her eyes had turned toward Gainsborough's studio, almost out of sight behind the trees. Perhaps it was natural for Alida to have an instinctive fear of Miss Ives. On the other hand, Ives seemed to be such a harmless person, even if she had lost Gains to Alida. Perhaps there was something more I needed to know about her, secrets within secrets. I hadn't found out, for example, why she was paying regular visits to a doctor.

I remembered something. Mrs. Howard got her knowledge, legendary in scope, of things medical from her niece who was head nurse at the convalescent home—the niece she went to visit once a month, the one she was so proud of. I wondered if she could be of use to me. It wouldn't hurt to try.

"There's one last thing, Mrs. H. Do you think you can get a list of every doctor in Briarcliff Manor, New York? Find out if any of them has a patient named Hope Ives or Hope Brown, or even Mrs. Oscar Brown. Make up some story. Say she's had a severe nervous breakdown and you're trying to track her down. Say she's been convalescing. Use anything that will work. And if you have any luck, try to find out what she's being treated for."

The prospect of long how-to-do-it consultations with her niece must have occurred to Mrs. Howard because her voice went husky with excitement. "You can count on me, Mrs. Willum."

"Don't forget—don't tell anyone I've left town. Not anyone."

"You can count on me." Mrs. Howard switched to a conspiratorial whisper. "Where are you going?"

"Not even you can know that," I said, playing it up big. "Good-bye. No one knows where I'm going but me, and nobody's going to know."

As I boarded the big Paris-bound jet, I sincerely hoped that I was right. Everything might depend on it.

Paris was unusually beautiful for September. The sky was such a cerulean blue, the still-blooming geraniums in the window box across the way were so very red, and the coffee and brioches of my breakfast had such a Paris smell that my old love affair with the city welled up within me and made me laugh out loud for pure joy. What a glorious way to wake up in the morning! I was tempted to forget my mission and spend the day wandering in the Tuileries gardens across from my hotel or strolling up the Champs Elysées. But no, all that would have to wait for another time—if there was to be another time.

I reached for the telephone.

Luck was with me on my very first call, which was to Alida's father. I found him listed in the book—Gérard du Prey. I was also fortunate enough to find him in when I telephoned and, after I explained that I was a friend of his daughter's, he agreed in the most polite and formal English to receive me after lunch. The conversation was short, and he expressed no curiosity about my call and asked no questions about his daughter. Nor did I volunteer anything. From the few words we exchanged, I was able to form no idea of what he would be like.

I next got in touch with Mme. Picarle, the French-woman I knew who had a small gallery on the Left Bank, so small that it was better compared to the shoehorn than to the shoe itself. But what treasures it contained! We had one of those friendly arrangements with her that are occasionally found among galleries all over the world: We sometimes exposed the work of her best painters and she would return the favor for ours. Gainsborough was the only one who scorned her; the facilities weren't grand enough for him. But others of our stable had experienced fantastic good luck in her hands, and I had the greatest faith in both her discretion and her connections.

I needed a very special favor, I told her, and she was the only person in all of France who could grant it in the time available. She was flattered, but it was no exaggeration. "Bien sûr."

Could she find out the particulars of a very peculiar sale that had taken place in Paris a month or so ago? It supposedly involved a Gainsborough Brown painting sold to benefit a penniless French painter. I paused.

Her reaction, heralded by a procession of small Gallic snorts of amusement, was identical to mine. "I will inquire around for you, but I can tell you this: Such a grand gesture does not fit the character of our friend Brown—not as I remember him. He was more likely, that one, to borrow their last sou from his penniless friends than to give anything to them!" She snorted again, this time derisively.

"Exactly," I said, very pleased that we were seeing eye-to-eye. Her skepticism was an asset, for if she said, in the end, that the story was true, I could be very sure that it was. "If Gains did do it, someone you know must have heard of it, no matter how they tried to keep it hushed up."

"There has been no gossip. Nevertheless, I shall get busy, never fear. Your friend Gainsborough spent enough time in Paris to have left a veritable mountain of ill will. Someone will talk if it really happened, be assured. A secret sale to benefit another artist—*formidable!* Almost a scandal! I will look into the affair and be in touch."

I spent the rest of the morning checking the individuals from whom Gregor had bought two of the Gainsborough Brown paintings in Paris. It took only a few telephone calls to confirm my suspicion that Gains had sold them both in order to pay debts and finance himself while he was courting Alida, and that Gregor had spent our Paris trip tracking them down and buying them back. The details regarding the third picture Gregor had sent back were still a mystery.

After a solitary lunch, I took a taxi to my appointment with Alida's father on the Ile Saint Louis, the little island which sits so serenely on the Seine, moored to the city and its bigger sister, the Ile de la Cité, by its rope of bridges.

M. du Prey's address was a fine seventeenth-century "hotel" with a walled-in cobbled courtyard and an impressive entrance hall. An elderly manservant in a striped waistcoat ushered me into a sitting room so small that I realized at once that if the house did indeed belong to the baron, he had long since divided it into apartments and kept only these rooms for himself. M. le Baron, I was told, would be with me in a moment, and I was quite content to wait, delighted as I was with my surroundings.

It was an octagonal salon of exquisite proportions, framed by pale grey boiseries. Could they be by Watteau? Did Watteau do decorative panels? I wished my aunt were here; she would know at a glance.

I noted several pieces of Louis XV furniture, including a

superb giltwood table. However, most of the furniture was of a far less distinguished vintage, and it sat around the room in the darkest corners, as if embarrassed to be present at all.

Four handsome snuff boxes caught my eye, sitting alone in a cabinet meant to display many more. Had their mates been sold? These were magnificent. One was made of bloodstone; another was gold-mounted and shaped like a shell. Even to my untutored eye they radiated quality.

Across the room stood a table covered with photographs—an incongruous touch, I thought, in this sophisticated atmosphere. There were dozens, standing in neat rows like perfectly regimented members of a drill team and displaying an astonishing variety of frame, from chased silver to walnut and ivory. There was even one with a stand made from boars' teeth.

I crossed over to look at them while I waited for my host.

"Ah, madame, I see that you enjoy my little family of photographs. It is an acquired taste for me, I must confess. My wife, like so many of her countrymen, had an enthusiasm for the camera, and my daughter inherited that taste."

I had not heard Gérard du Prey come into the room; now he was bowing over my hand. "I am delighted that you have honored me with this visit."

What had I expected of Alida's father? Had I thought he would be stern? Or cold? Whatever I expected, it was not the man who faced me now.

Oh, there was a resemblance to his daughter. They had the same grey eyes, the same fineness of bone. But there was a refinement in him that Alida didn't quite achieve. He combined strength with a delicacy of structure, in that beautiful and manly compatibility one finds only in the French.

Had I thought he would be old? He could have been her brother. His face was scarcely lined and his blue-black hair was only beginning to go grey, enough of a hint of age to be fascinating—so fascinating that for the first time in a long time, I felt nervous about being alone in a room with a man.

I turned to the photographs to cover my confusion. "I'm afraid it's a taste I've acquired, too. Are there any here of Alida? She must have been a lovely child."

"Most of them are of Alida." He leaned over my shoulder, and I caught the faint smell of the scent he used. "There—my daughter when she was an infant, in London."

"London?"

"Her mother was English, you know. Alida lived in England with her grandparents after her mother died until I brought her back. Her mother died when she was born. I'm afraid it was a lonely household for one little girl living alone with one busy man, even with Thérèse. After all, Thérèse couldn't take the place of a mother, although she tried."

So Alida was part English. That accounted for what Oliver had called her "milkmaid" quality.

"Thérèse?" I asked.

"Her nurse. She was nurse to my wife during her last illness, and she felt such pity for the motherless baby that she stayed on. Too long, really. You will find many pictures of Thérèse, too. She was always with my daughter."

He pointed out a photograph of a woman in a bulky black coat holding a young Alida by the hand. The child's eyes stared straight at the camera, and she was smiling prettily.

"What became of Thérèse?"

Du Prey shrugged. "She married, finally. Some ne'er-do-well who fancied himself an artist, if I remember. That class often makes disastrous marriages." He smiled at me so warmly that I forgave him his small touch of snobbery. "Here." Reaching among the frames, he selected a special one. "The last picture I have of my daughter and Thérèse together, taken just before Thérèse left us."

I bent over the photograph, at first just pretending to look at it and then suddenly staring hard. I didn't want to contradict my host, but it was not the last picture of the two of them together. Unquestionably there was a more recent one, in Gainsborough Brown's wooden box, wherever that was now. Here was Thérèse in partial profile and the likeness was unmistakable: She was the same woman as the one in the *Match* photo of Alida at the Young Americans show in Paris.

"I hope my daughter is well?"

"She isn't, unfortunately. She has been under a doctor's care since her husband's death."

"I am sorry to hear that." It was perfunctory. He wasn't really interested. "I suppose she told you that I was absolutely opposed to her marriage?"

I nodded.

"I hoped that she would respect my wishes. But my daughter was never ... easy. Ah, well." He turned away gracefully and gestured toward a chair. "Enough of this. I do not wish to bore such a charming guest. We must have a glass of champagne to celebrate your visit. Pierre!"

The manservant appeared instantly, bringing a bottle of Pol Roger and two long-stemmed crystal "flutes." Du Prey raised his glass to me. "It is my most sincere wish, now that we have met, that my daughter's friend will be mine, too. I do not wish to lose you." His eyes met mine, and the momentary anger I'd felt at his lack of concern for Alida vanished. His compliment was most disarming and very personal.

"Thank you. I am delighted to be here. But tell me"—I wanted to change the subject, as I couldn't allow myself to respond this way to a man I'd just met—"why were you opposed to the marriage? In America he was quite a famous person."

"Famous?" He gave me a curious glance. "Perhaps that was his appeal." He began to twist his glass around and around on the table before him. "He wasn't suitable, to answer your question. He was the antithesis of everything I and the people of my class represent—if one can speak of class today!"

He stood up and went to the window, speaking with his

135

back to me as if to conceal his emotion. "No, he was unsuitable. In fact, he was a savage. No taste, no background. She may have thought he had money. Certainly we never had enough of it, and I could almost have forgiven her if that was the case. He made a great display of extravagance. But when he asked me bluntly about Alida's financial prospects and I made it clear to him that I was not a rich man, I thought it would be the end of the affair. My daughter would be angry, but she would recover." He came back and touched the champagne bottle absently to assure himself that it was still cold.

"Then what happened?"

"Who can say? I thought I had discouraged him. Then suddenly they were married and I did not see them again. But no more of that. Now we will talk about you." He leaned forward on the arm of the delicate little sofa and looked at me intently. "How long will you be here? I should like to show you my Paris if you will permit me."

"I'm only here through tomorrow," I said. "I am on a quick visit to my aunt, Lydia Wentworth." I don't know why I mentioned her name, but he reacted so quickly that I might have dropped a live grenade in his lap. Everything changed. Gone was the atmosphere of romance, the unspoken promises and `the feeling that I was the only attractive woman in the world.

"When you see that lovely lady, will you please tell her that Gérard du Prey sends his devoted sentiments?" His voice was very correct.

"You know her, monsieur?" I stood up to leave. Alida's father rose, too.

"I knew her once. The world turns in very small circles indeed, madame. It has been a pleasure to meet you."

He bowed over my hand once more and the interview was finished.

Mme. Picarle had dinner with me in my room that evening. She told me she had definitely established that, to her intense surprise, the story about Gainsborough's selling one of his pictures as an act of charity was, to all appearances, true.

Her information was that Gains had approached one of the very good galleries on the Faubourg St. Honoré and offered them the opportunity of selling one of the best works of his earlier period. True, it wasn't signed, but the gallery accepted his story about his intention to break his contract with Gregor as a reasonable excuse, inasmuch as Gains guaranteed to furnish shortly either his signature or proof of authenticity. Gains insisted on three conditions: First, the picture must be sold within two weeks; second, Gains's share of any monies accruing were to be deposited to the account of a certain French citizen; third, there was to be complete secrecy—no details were ever to be made public.

However, the gallery owner considered it such an acquisition that he purchased the work himself on behalf of his firm. After a few weeks, he began quietly showing his new acquisition to his more important clients. Naturally, he attached a healthy markup.

"Were you able to find out who got the price of the original sale?" I asked.

"A certain Jules Toussant, and we can tell you a great deal about him—except where he is now." My friend had been a member of the Résistance, and her connections from those days still penetrated every fiber of Parisian life.

Jules Toussant, it seems, with a past history as a forger, had spent the war years as an expert at furnishing false documents, identities and passports. In those days, no one quibbled about how a man acquired his special talents. There was some suspicion that he had dealt with both sides, but it was only a suspicion and was never proven. At the end of the Occupation, he had drifted from one thing to another, trying a variety of careers without success. Lately he had been calling himself an artist.

"I see." I only wished it were true. "What do you suppose it all means?"

"He is forging art, of course, what else? But there is

more. Our old training makes us thorough. About two years ago he married a certain Thérèse Marat. Thérèse Marat was the nurse of Alida du Prey, whom Gainsborough Brown married."

So! The thread had unwound all the way from Gainsborough's wooden box to Paris and back again!

"And one last thing that I think will interest you. . . ." My friend was proud of the job she had done on such short notice. She lit a Gauloise and casually blew a few rings of smoke in quick succession. "The owner of the gallery learned that a certain American gentleman was interested in any Gainsborough Browns that might be on the market, so he sent a message to the gentleman's hotel. The following morning the picture was sold for seventy-nine thousand dollars to this gentleman at a fine profit." The mystery of the third painting had been solved. This *was* the third painting.

"And the gentleman was Gregor Olitsky!" There wasn't any doubt in my mind. "But . . . what became of the Toussants?"

"It would seem that the marriage was not a success because she left him in some haste to be nurse to a family now cruising in the Greek Islands. I am told she gave every indication of wanting to get as far away from him as possible. As to Jules Toussant, who knows? A man like that could disappear without a trace. But we are working on it."

"If you find him, please let me know. Even a photograph . . ."

She looked at me and sighed. That sigh spoke volumes. A Jules Toussant, it said, would he leave photographs lying around? Such a man, schooled in all the arts of deception, living by his wits—would he be such a fool?

But she was very polite. "If a photograph exists, you shall have it," she promised. *"A bientôt."*

"A bientôt. Et milles mercis."

I was not depressed—far from it. As I had suspected, the missing pieces of the puzzle were turning up in Paris, with Jules Toussant being one of them. Now all I had to do was put the pieces together.

17

The next morning I was out of the hotel and in a taxi by eight fifteen. I was hoping to surprise Aunt Lydie by arriving at the Avenue Raphaël when I was certain she'd still be in bed. That is, if she was there at all.

It was going to be another glorious day, one of those when the people on the sidewalks and those cycling along in the traffic look pleased to be on their way to work. So different from the grim commuters I saw on Long Island. A workman on a bicycle with his ladder strapped to his back was wedged into the traffic like a cork in a bottle, but he saluted me cheerfully as we passed in the opposite direction. Two gendarmes, immaculately uniformed and moustached, cycled along side by side. Sparkles of sunshine bounced on the waters of the fountains. The plane trees waved their arms in leafy abandon. The buildings looked marvelously white and clean. I couldn't help feeling pleased with myself for being part of this scene.

The taxi pulled up before a superb early-nineteenth-century townhouse, and I asked the driver to wait. Early morning rock and roll, French style, followed me from the cab radio as I ran up the granite steps and rang the bell. My aunt's maid, Hannah, answered in person. I was in luck once more.

"Miss Persis! I don't believe it! What are you doing in Paris?"

"Mad as it may seem, I made a quick trip over to visit Aunt Lydie. Is she in?"

"She's having her breakfast. Come upstairs and surprise her."

I motioned the taxi to go, and I followed Hannah into the house.

"Miss Wentworth is going to be really startled to see you," Hannah was saying as she led me down the hall and up the stairs. "I can't imagine how you found us. She's done everything to keep her whereabouts a secret—even putting the phone in the maid's name. She hasn't seen anyone at all."

I noticed as we passed that the entrance hall and the two salons to the right were in a state of upheaval, with bolts of material draped over furniture and swathed temporarily over windows. Pictures and mirrors stood on the floor, leaning against the walls with their faces turned in. My aunt was in the process of moving either out or in, but I couldn't decide which.

All of this I took in with more or less half an eye as we moved along. Mainly I was busy wondering in what mood I would find my aunt and whether I would have the nerve to ask her if she knew why Gains had married Alida, as Miss Ives had implied she did. People like Lydia Wentworth weren't like ordinary mortals: You could fly all the way to Paris to ask a specific question and be intimidated out of saying a single word when they looked at you.

When we entered her room, I could tell from the huskiness of her voice when she greeted me that she was barely awake. "Why, Persis, this is a surprise!" She was speaking from somewhere deep in the back of her throat. "Would you like some coffee? It's French. Have you had breakfast? Hannah, ring for something for Mrs. Willum, please."

Seen in the morning light before she had really been out of bed, my aunt was a miracle of preservation. Her skin glowed with the elasticity of youth. I guess if she lived to be a hundred she would always be a tearing beauty—one of nature's great phenomena.

It was typical of her immense style that right this minute she wasn't asking what I was doing in her bedroom in Paris when nobody was even supposed to know she was here. She must have known perfectly well that I hadn't tracked her down and come all this way for nothing, but she didn't ask. And faced with her aplomb, I couldn't blurt out the question I'd come to have answered, at least not without some preliminaries.

"You know, Aunt Lydie, I was worried about you. No one knew where you were staying over here and you weren't registered at your usual hotels. I thought you might be hiding, but I wasn't sure."

I shouldn't have said that last bit. She became quite flustered. "What do you mean, hiding? Hide? I'm not hiding. What on earth would I be hiding from?"

"I'm sorry," I said. "I meant that you might be running away from all the publicity about Gains's death. I know how you hate newspapers and fuss."

That made her relax. "You're perfectly right about that part of it. Hannah, are they bringing Mrs. Willum something? Yes, the publicity would have been more than I could face. Especially since I actually had nothing to do with that dreadful young man except having him die in my pool. And I didn't invite him to do that, after all."

She waved a ring-laden hand at me. I wondered if she slept with her jewels on or if she put them on before breakfast. The morning light was striking fire from a fortune in gems on her small, perfectly shaped fingers. "And he was a dreadful young man, much as I hate to say it. Put it down right there, Hannah, and then you can leave us."

She watched me measure out the right mixture of milk and sugar for the strong French coffee. Then she nibbled and poked about at her own breakfast, pretending to be engrossed in eating but really watching me out of the corner of her eye all the time. She was waiting for me to

141

state my business; and I thrashed around mentally, trying to decide how to lead into my question. Maybe if I began with Gérard du Prey and worked my way to the marriage by stages . . .

"I went to visit the Baron du Prey yesterday," I ventured. "You never told me that you knew Alida's father. What a charming man! He sent you his devotion. I think that was the word he used."

At the mention of du Prey's name she had set her coffee cup down with a clatter that made the china and the jam jars on the silver tray rattle. "So that's it! I suspected the minute you walked in this door. After all, why else would you be in Paris?" She picked up her napkin and began to wave it at me. "I suppose you got wind of the trouble and rushed right over here and persuaded Gérard to tell you everything, as if I couldn't take care of myself, at my age. I thought I'd handled it very well."

"Aunt Lydie . . ." I began, dumbfounded.

"Of course, that's why you're here! Don't tell me you ran over to Paris to have breakfast with me?"

"Why, no. Actually, I was wondering about Alida and . . ."

"Exactly!" She sighed. "Well, it doesn't matter now. I don't know why I let myself get so excited. But I had hoped to keep it quiet. I suppose Gérard told you everything you hadn't already guessed. I must say, I thought he could be trusted this once. It is his daughter!"

This time I was determined to interrupt. I had to defend that poor man. "All he ever said was that he sent his devotion. He never said another word, Aunt Lydie."

"Oh." She lowered her lashes and gave me a mischievous glance. It was amazing how quickly she could change gear. "Isn't he attractive? I mean, he used to be. I haven't seen him for years."

"He is—very."

"Of course, being attractive is a sort of profession with him. But still . . ." She looked pleased. "He has great charm, hasn't he? And he sent me . . ."

"His devotion. I had the impression that he has more than a little twinge for you."

I might have been mistaken, but I thought she blushed. "Did he really seem, you know, about me?"

I nodded.

"Still? Well, I'm glad. I was afraid when you first came in that I was going to have to give him money so he wouldn't talk and I would have hated that, even though there was no truth in any of it. He's always been something of a cad, I'm afraid. But I have a weakness for them—cads are so much more fun than the regular types." She shifted gears once more. "I'm glad he didn't say anything. I think I can finish my breakfast now."

She did just that, down to the very last crumb—daintily but thoroughly. She did it with such enjoyment that I knew Gérard du Prey's silence had pleased her very much, whatever it was he had been silent about. I waited quietly, sipping my coffee. I knew my aunt. She was in a good mood now. She would tell me more; she would tell me what I had come to ask without my ever asking. But only when she was ready.

"Well," she said, examining the empty plates with satisfaction. "Since you already know so much, I suppose I may as well tell you the rest."

I tried to appear as well informed as she assumed I was, meanwhile wondering *what* it was that I knew.

It seems she had first been introduced to the baron just after the war when he was in New York "doing things," as she put it, with various committees to help the French get themselves reorganized.

"Naturally, we met. I was on every committee in those days. Everyone knew I was a dedicated Francophile, so I couldn't say 'no' to anything. Anyway, I like to be sure that I'm giving my money in ways that really help. I like to see to it personally."

That was one way of putting it. There were plenty of

people who said it was easier to get a dollar out of Fort Knox than out of Aunt Lydie. She was notoriously tight-fisted.

Gérard du Prey had cut a romantic figure. He was fresh from the rigors of the Occupation, heartbreakingly lean and hungry-looking, desperately handsome and well endowed with Gallic allure. They were thrown together a good deal; in fact, they saw each other constantly. It was inevitable that they would fall in love, considering Aunt Lydie's amorous proclivities.

"I followed him back to France. There was no question of letting him go without me. How could I settle for any of the American men I knew? After all, Gérard *was* France. To me he was what the war was all about. I was in a state of real enchantment. You know what I mean—you are in a room full of people, but you see only one. When he comes through a doorway unexpectedly, you think your heart will burst. It's always so lovely." She ought to know. It was said she had been in love so many times that it was a state of mind with her. I admired the way she could still look wistful.

"Yes," she sighed. "It's always so thrilling. You know, I do believe it's good for one."

"You may be right." And it did occur to me that all those romances may be the reason she stayed so beautiful, thriving on the certainty that love is ever a joy. Unlike me, who has let herself get so soured on the subject.

"I'm sure I am." She jutted her chin out for emphasis. "It's the feeling that's so salubrious, and one must never stop to be intellectual about it. Because the most attractive men seldom stand up under close scrutiny. One must simply enjoy them for what they are and then forget them. Never, never be serious and Wagnerian about love. Gérard was a perfect example of what I mean."

She sighed. I couldn't say whether it was with pleasure or with regret.

"I had no intention of marrying Gérard. I knew he was a little unreliable. It was clearly understood by both of us that it was just a temporary madness. I remember telling myself that there might not be more of these madnesses left to me. After all, I was at the wrong end of my thirties at the time." She laughed, and I joined her. The thought that she would turn into an old hag on the stroke of forty was a joke, as twenty-five years had passed since she turned forty, and she wasn't hag-like yet.

But after the flash of laughter she grew serious again.

"It didn't last long, in any event. You know how I always get sick when I am in Paris, Persis. I think it's the dampness. It happens every time, and still I can't stop coming because I love the city so. Today, for instance, I was planning to stay in bed. I think I may have a cold coming on even though the weather is so beautiful."

My aunt stirred restlessly. She hated illness, and I knew that if she even had to see the dentist, she did it in complete secrecy. Anything short of absolute physical perfection wasn't acceptable to her.

"You were ill, weren't you?" I vaguely remembered that there had been a time when I was a little girl when my aunt was in the hospital in Paris.

"At first I thought it was nothing—*un petit rhume.* I didn't have time to be ill at the moment, as you can imagine, and I didn't trust French doctors. I still don't. So I neglected myself and landed in the American Hospital with pneumonia. While I was there I learned that Gérard had kept from me the fact that he was married and that, curiously, his wife was in the same hospital. She had given birth to a child—a little girl—and there were complications. While I was still there, she died. You can imagine my feelings. Naturally, it was the end of the affair."

My aunt rang for another cup of coffee. She didn't drink it when it arrived; she merely stirred it, moving the spoon around and around in the cup while her rings flashed in the sunlight. The clink of the silver against the china was the only sound in the room for several minutes.

"It's so incredible, I still don't believe it," she said finally. "Maybe you can understand. You did seem to get along with that young man, Gainsborough Brown. I confess that there were even moments when I wondered if you had anything to do with it. But I decided it was impossible . . . I don't suppose Gérard told you?"

"Told me what?"

"Good. You see it did involve his daughter, after all. Well," she drew a long breath, "Gainsborough Brown came to see me shortly after he and his wife were married and demanded a great deal of money. He said that if I didn't produce it—and it was a shocking sum—I would find myself involved in a scandal so dreadful that I would never want to be seen in public again. Not," she sniffed, "that I care about being seen in public."

It was incredible. It was appalling. It was insane. Imagine anyone, even Gainsborough, saying such a thing to my aunt! "What did you say?" I demanded.

"Naturally, I ordered him out of the house. I told him that if he needed money, all he had to do was apply himself to his easel. Plenty of people, I understood, were waiting to buy his work, though," she felt obliged to add, "I don't know why. I was very cross with young Mr. Brown, but it never occurred to me that he could be serious. I know how difficult artists can be, and I suspected that his pride was hurt because I would never buy one of his pictures. Yes, I was irritated but not alarmed."

"You should have called Gregor, Aunt Lydie."

"I never thought of it. But several days later I had a call from one of the columnists, one that traffics in innuendo rather than fact. The conversation upset me. She kept asking me what I planned to do about what had happened in Paris after the war and if I had a statement at this time. Then Brown appeared again. He had some photographs. One was an old clipping of me with Gérard du Prey, and another was of a woman he said was nursing Gérard's wife when she died. He told me this woman was alive and prepared to testify that Gérard's wife did not die in childbirth; that she had died as a result of a miscarriage suffered months before. He then produced a legal document, a photostat of an *extrait de naissance,* which said that the child Alida had been born to me—*me*—in the American Hospital in Paris in 1950."

I stared at her, aghast.

"I know," she said. "It defies the imagination. I couldn't believe my ears and I most certainly couldn't believe my eyes. The documents looked absolutely genuine, smothered in stamps and seals and things. They looked so genuine that for the moment I forgot that Alida's birth would be registered in the Mairie de Neuilly and could be checked."

"How terrible!" I cried. "Why would he want to do such a crazy thing?"

Aunt Lydie shrugged. "Why does anyone do anything dishonest? For love or money, of course. In this case, money. He figured it all out very carefully. If I'd kept it a secret all these years that I had a daughter, he said, it ought to be worth a lot to continue keeping it a secret. He had the nerve to tell me that if I paid him a reasonable amount now, he was quite willing to wait until I was dead for his wife to claim her estate. If I didn't pay him, he would make the whole thing public immediately."

"Why didn't you notify the police?"

"Are you mad? Don't you know the newspapers would have had it in two minutes? And true or false, it certainly would have made a scandal, especially since he was married to my supposed daughter. That poor child—can you imagine a worse mess? And can you imagine my mixed feelings when I met her for the first time at my birthday party?"

I couldn't. "But why would he take a chance of involving his wife in something so unpleasant?"

"Where money was at stake, I doubt that he ever gave a thought to anyone's sensibilities. At least, that was my impression."

I thought I could imagine what happened next. "You got in touch with Gérard, didn't you?"

"Of course. It was the logical thing. Ordinarily, I don't approve of telephoning transatlantic—a definite extravagance. Miss Styles doesn't understand. If she had her way, she would be calling me every single day from New York. *No* idea of the value of money! But in this case, the circumstances were decidedly exceptional, so I telephoned Gérard. I wasn't even certain that he was alive, but he was; and he was horrified. But, I had a distinct feeling that he wasn't too terribly surprised. He made no secret of the fact that he didn't think much of Gainsborough Brown."

My aunt had pushed her coffee aside untasted. She now paused to study the white and gold pattern of the cup with great interest, as if she were seeing it for the first time. "I never exactly thought of Gérard as the soul of honor, but blackmail is something else again! I had the impression that he was truly shocked! The nuances of morality are very complicated, aren't they? At any rate, he checked the Mairie and called me back to assure me that the genuine records were available and that I could jail Gainsborough Brown for blackmail if I wished to prosecute. Of course, I preferred to settle the matter myself, both for the sake of his poor daughter and for my own sake. Without publicity."

"And you did?"

"Naturally. Without paying anyone a penny." This was said with great satisfaction and in a tone that indicated that the subject was now closed. She picked up her coffee cup, changed her mind, set it down again with a small crash and rang for Hannah. "Where are you stopping, Persis? We might have lunch tomorrow."

"I'm going back tomorrow."

She didn't say anything, but her eyes widened, and I knew she was thinking how profligate to spend my hard-earned dollars on transatlantic sleuthing. Yet she hadn't questioned me.

Hannah came in just then, very trim in her neat black dress, and went off to draw Aunt Lydie's bath. Wasn't it odd, I thought, that the people who serve the rich so often grow to look like the rich themselves? Certainly Hannah, whose face contained just the right mixture of aristocratic

148

bones, could have passed among them anywhere. She had the right patina.

My aunt saw me watching her. "I can't imagine what I shall do if she ever retires. She knows exactly how I like everything. She's promised she won't unless . . ." Then came the characteristic abrupt change of subject, which was anything but capricious. "How is Gregor?"

"He wants me to ask if he could borrow the birthday-present sculpture Gainsborough gave you to show in conjunction with a fund-raising . . ."

To my surprise, she brushed it aside. I had never thought she'd consent. "I'll tell Miss Styles that you will pick it up." A look of mild distaste crept over her face. "I wish I could lend it to him forever. I don't consider it part of my collection; it was an unsolicited addition." She slid over to the edge of the bed, poking her foot around on the floor in search of a slipper. "And Gregor . . . how is he?"

"I don't know, Aunt Lydie. To be perfectly honest, I think he hasn't been himself ever since we were in Paris together."

The foot stopped its probing and hung in midair. "Ahhh!" The petulant lines of her face slowly dissolved and the corners of her mouth began to curve upward. "Would you say he was . . ." she pondered the choice of a word, ". . . unhappy?"

"And angry with the world, I guess. Something's bothering him."

She was openly smiling when, just then, Hannah appeared and announced that the bath was ready. My aunt waved her away impatiently and went on smiling like a woman who was enjoying a huge, private joke. I began to get vibrations from that smile, faint at first and then very, very strong.

"Aunt Lydie," I said, speaking much louder than I had intended to, "what's wrong with Gregor, anyway?"

She threw her head back and let loose her merriment. "He's furious because I'm not going to marry him after all, at least I don't think I am. Imagine—he wouldn't even

149

come to my birthday party, so what could he expect? Do close your mouth, Persis, you look foolish. Don't you agree that everyone should be married at least once in a lifetime?"

———

I stumbled out of the house on the Avenue Raphaël and walked along the sidewalk without the vaguest idea of where I was going or why. All I knew was that I had to think for a while.

Gregor had proposed to Aunt Lydie and she had accepted—that much was definite. And Hannah had confided in me on the way out that my aunt had bought this house as a wedding gift to Gregor, to be their European headquarters once the Paris gallery opened.

But Gregor foolishly hadn't turned up for her birthday gala. Then he had heaped insult upon injury by suggesting that she invest in his galleries. (This proposal came in a letter forwarded by Miss Styles, since Aunt Lydie had refused to speak to him after he missed her party.) Actually, Hannah's threat of retirement could have been the final blow, although my aunt would never have admitted it.

"She may go back to him yet," Hannah had whispered to me at the top of the stairs. "She's torn this house apart and redecorated it three times. I've never known her to be so extravagant. Everything has been remonogrammed, and what she can't find here she orders from New York. We all wish she'd make up her mind! The strain is killing us!"

I didn't believe any of it, though. Lydia Wentworth would never marry. Gregor had caught her on a bad day, when she was feeling feeble and theorizing that everyone ought to be married at least once.

No. The main thing to think about was Gainsborough Brown and his blackmail scheme. Mind-boggling, it was. Quite obviously Alida's nurse, Thérèse, and her husband, Jules Toussaint, had smelled a nice opportunity to make money when Gainsborough Brown appeared on the du Prey horizon trumpeting his acquaintance with Lydia

150

Wentworth in an effort to impress the du Preys. It must have gone like this: Jules would forge the documents and offer them, along with Thérèse's testimony, for sale to Gainsborough for a very large sum of money. They must also have sniffed out Gains's greed, for if there was one thing Gains believed, it was that if something cost enough, it had to be worthwhile. The price of the painting was Jules's payoff.

And, until my aunt telephoned him, Gérard du Prey never understood why Gainsborough Brown suddenly married his daughter just when he thought he had discouraged him by explaining that his child was not an heiress. What would Gains have done to Miss Ives if Alida had really been Aunt Lydie's daughter? I hated to think. And what had he done to Alida herself when he found it wasn't true? Was that the reason for the bruises on her arms? Poor Alida.

I walked along the sidewalk like a sleepwalker. One thing, at least, I thought, makes sense in all this madness. No wonder Aunt Lydie had warned me not to think of Gregor in terms of marriage. She had been considering it herself!

18

The last part of the plane trip back was rough—the residue, we were informed, of a storm that had battered the East Coast the night before, causing the first hurricane alert of the season. Seat belts stayed fastened until we made a sun-drenched but rocky landing.

On the ground evidences of the storm were visible everywhere. Roads were crisscrossed with downed trees; stalled and abandoned cars dotted the landscape; and maintenance crews were at work on all sides, swarming up and down utility poles with the industry of ants. That indefatigable Cassandra, the car radio, punctuated my drive home with reports that five more deaths had been attributed to the storm and that most of the one hundred forty thousand homeowners affected by the power failure would remain without electricity throughout the night despite round-the-clock repair efforts.

I didn't need the radio to tell me that Gull Harbor and its environs had been hard hit. My own driveway, when I arrived, was a mess of leaves and branches, and my favorite elm tree was down, having neatly missed the side of the house. I had been worrying all the way home about my basement. If it had flooded, the sump pump wouldn't operate with the electricity out, and it was surely flooded if the still-standing lake of storm water in front of the house could be believed. That anything more disastrous than a flooded basement could have happened never entered my mind.

Mrs. Howard wasn't in the house. She had left fresh candles in every candleholder, and she had also left a note: "Telephone kaput. Radio says train out, but North Port has all services; so I'm hitching a ride to my niece's to finish telephone calls there. Seven doctors to go. Casserole in oven. Thank goodness for gas! Back tonight."

I had an instant vision of her standing on the road that ran past my house, her square-cut hair on end from the wind, her small body as challenging as an Indian's lance planted in the ground. The very first passing car would pick her up—no need to worry.

I put the note down, still smiling to myself at the industry with which Mrs. Howard was pursuing her investigations, and headed for the kitchen, where I peered into the cellar, never doubting that it would be awash. Past storms had established a sort of floating pecking order for the objects that lived down there: First would come wicker porch furniture that Blackstone never got around to repairing, bobbing and nodding like old ladies on a veranda at Cape May; then a gardening glove or two, soggy hands without arms; bunches of bamboo stakes left over from the cutting garden; and then the plastic mats that normally sat in front of the washing machine and dryer. All these things—and more—would be sailing past the fourth step from the bottom. The first three steps would be under water.

I lit one of the candles and aimed in into the murky darkness below. All was in order. A white chair sailed slowly into view. I shut the basement door with an angry bang. No electricity, no sump pump, and what looked like a five-step flood! Welcome home!

A quick check of the oven came next. Mrs. Howard's casserole sat inside, regal in aluminum foil.

Then upstairs to my bedroom, carrying my overnight bag. A stack of telephone messages lay on my bedside table, and I reminded myself to glance at them before it came time to light the candles. Newspapers from the past two days were lying on a chair under a small stack of mail. I caught a glimpse of the morning's headline—STORM BATTERS EAST COAST. There would be time for all that after a relaxing warm bath (as Mrs. Howard said, thank goodness for gas!) and just the smallest of naps—five minutes or so.

It was dark when the pounding on my door woke me. I groped for the candle Mrs. Howard had left on the table and struck a light. Dreamily as Lady Macbeth I descended the stairs, candle aloft. That was Mrs. Howard banging on the door. And someone was with her—I vaguely heard a second voice.

"You got the door bolted on the inside, Mrs. Willum!" Mrs. Howard's tone was loud and reproachful.

"Persis, Persis, let us in!" That was Oliver, the second voice, and he sounded anxious.

They squeezed in side by side, both talking at once, Mrs. Howard explaining that Oliver had picked her up while she was waiting for a ride from the village and Oliver saying that he had been on his way to check on me anyway. Without pausing to take off her coat and boots, Mrs. Howard began to light candles all over the house, whispering "Bingo!" to herself in a meaningful tone. I got the impression that she was trying to tell me something.

Oliver ignored her. "I thought I ought to check on you, Persis, especially after what happened last night."

"Really, Oliver," I yawned. "A little wind and rain . . . we've had worse storms than this before!"

"I wasn't thinking about the storm. I was afraid the other business would upset you."

"What other business?" He really was behaving as if I were a mental invalid!

"Haven't you heard? Didn't you read the paper? Hasn't anyone told you?" He sounded incredulous.

"What are you talking about, Oliver? I haven't read the papers, and with the telephone out, how could anyone tell

154

me anything?" An apprehensive cramp stirred in my stomach.

Oliver had a newspaper under his arm. He handed it to me now. "It's all in there. I thought of course you knew by now. Very sad business, Persis. Eleanore de Pauw was killed last night in an accident."

I read the cold words by the light of the warm candles:

NORTH SHORE SOCIALITE DEAD IN STORM
Eleanore de Pauw, 57. . . .

My own candle shook and dimmed in my hand. Oliver tried to take it from me, but I didn't let him. "No, no . . . I'm all right. Leave me alone. I have to read it!"

She had left the house sometime during the storm and set out for Oak Hill. No one could establish the time exactly. Dickie had left earlier on a tour of friends' houses to "round up storm supplies." The servants hadn't heard her go.

She was on the last leg of the drive to Oak Hill, which was situated at the end of a section of private road that wound in and out along the shore. At a point where the road turned sharply to avoid the harbor inlet she had failed to make the turn and plunged straight into the water. That she should have missed the corner was a puzzle. She herself had insisted on the placing of a large warning arrow in that very spot despite the objections of several committee-women who felt that it would spoil the scenic beauty of the road. Police theorized that she had not seen the arrow until too late because of the storm. She had been driving fast and her brakes would have been wet.

There was more—about her work with the Historical Society and the history of the restoration of Oak Hill—but I didn't read it all. I couldn't. I felt too sick.

"I've been by to see old Dickie," Oliver was saying. "He's all broken up, poor thing. Says he had no idea she'd go screaming off—as he put it—to look at Oak Hill in the middle of a storm. Says she was always worried about the place flooding but didn't realize she was worried enough to drive in that kind of weather."

The newspaper suddenly weighed a ton. I handed it back to Oliver. "Did she say anything to the servants?"

"Not a thing, according to Dickie. They told him there were one or two phone calls just before the telephone went out that she answered herself. But that's all. The storm was making so much noise they never heard her leave."

Telephone calls. I had made a call to her from Alida's house three days ago. I had left a message, one that had been written down. And suddenly there was a turn she shouldn't have missed on a road she shouldn't have been on. I must have looked as strange as I felt because Oliver was calling to Mrs. Howard, and then he had his arms around me and was moving me gently toward the stairs. "Mrs. Howard, let's get her to bed, shall we? This has been a shock."

I wished they would leave me alone. "Please . . . I don't need any help." I felt like a puppet being jerked this way and that.

Oliver's face was an eyelash away from mine. "I don't suppose you've seen a doctor yet?"

"What for? I don't need a doctor," I cried, furiously.

There was a sudden explosion of light. The little world around us came alive in one eye-blinding instant as the electricity came on and we were out of the darkness. It caught Oliver's face by surprise, caught it wearing a look of deepest speculation, caught him in mid-sentence. "Eleanore, our unfortunate Eleanore. I suppose you could say she was the type who noticed things?"

Mrs. Howard had the final word. "Not no more, she don't," she pronounced grimly.

———

Much later Mrs. Howard told me about her telephone calls. We were unpacking, and she prolonged the suspense of her report by dashing in and out of the bathroom with toilet articles between sentences.

"Never did get hold of Mrs. de Pauw before she died.

156

Lucky thing my niece's telephones didn't go out, with all them doctors still left to call . . . which reminds me, you got a stack of calls yourself before we was blacked out. And I'll tell you this, I didn't know there were so many doctors in one place. Thought I never would get done. And then, just when I'd about run out of them, bingo!"

"Bingo?" How exasperating of her! Why couldn't she get to the point?

"I wrote the kind he was down and memorized it so I'd be sure to get it right." Her voice squeaked with excitement and pride.

"Get *what* right, Mrs. Howard?"

But she would not be rushed. "There was this one doctor, not even listed in the book because he's semi-retired. Very clever of Miss Ives to pick him. But my niece remembered him from when they were both at White Plains Hospital, so she got the number. And, would you believe, he was the one."

There was nothing to do but grit my teeth while she made a couple of extra trips to intensify the suspense. Finally she couldn't stand it any more herself. She took a stand in the middle of the room, cleared her throat importantly, and told me.

"This doctor is an ophthalmologist and I talked to his nurse. She says Miss Ives came to them about three years ago with eyes that were practically falling out of her head from 'prolonged strain and working under artificial lights.' I got it all right here," Mrs. Howard said, tapping the side of her head dramatically. "She should have been wearing those really heavy glasses. But the nurse says for some reason she never got the prescription filled, and they didn't see her again until recently. Now she needs glasses thick enough to drive a tank over if she's going to see at all."

"Oh." And she hadn't wanted me to know. She had lied outright.

"One thing more. Somebody did leave something here. Hardrock finally got his brains together and remembered that Gainsborough Brown left a bunch of framed posters in the toolshed. I looked them over good, knowing you was looking for something dramatic, but that's all they are—posters. What do you think of that?"

She had asked a good question. What, indeed, did I think of that? Later I would go out and examine the posters myself and find that she was absolutely right—that's all they were. But they had most certainly been dramatic the night Gains looked at them in front of Susan Evans.

The small parish church of Gull Harbor had never been built to accommodate as many people as those who came to the services for Eleanore de Pauw. The very stones of its staid Episcopal walls groaned from the pressure of the crowds inside. I recognized Tillson, the builder to whom she had faithfully given the contracts for her restorations over the years, and his wife, who was beside him, properly mournful in head-to-toe black except for her gloves, which were short and freshly laundered white. Tillson would miss Eleanore. The Gull Harbor druggist was there, too, peering sideways from lowered eyes to spot his customers in the crowd. The grocer, the liquor dealer, the editor of the Gull Harbor *Weekly*, the mayor. Most of the faces were familiar.

I was late, as usual—this time because I couldn't find a place to park—and by the time I had eased myself into the last seat of the last pew at the rear of the church, the Reverend Dr. Markham Synge was embarking on the opening lines of "The Lord is my shepherd; therefore can I lack nothing."

Instantly, and as if the words had been a signal, I began to cry. It was frightening and humiliating (we don't cry at funerals in Gull Harbor—stoicism is *de rigueur*), but I couldn't stop.

"Surely Thy loving-kindness and mercy shall follow me all the days of my life: and I will dwell in the house of the Lord forever."

The tears kept flowing. People around me had begun to stir and glance sideways in my direction. A few in the rows ahead looked back. I couldn't stop. It was like a nightmare.

I wept through psalms, hymns, the Apostles' Creed and a prayer. And I knew I wasn't going to stop. How could I when I was sure—absolutely sure—that this woman was dead because I'd left a telephone message pointing her out to a killer? No good telling myself I couldn't have known how it would turn out.

The church door was right next to me. I slipped out and rested my forehead against the cool bark of the tree that nestled against the stone and shaded the entrance. My breathing got back to normal.

Inside the church, the organ heralded the singing of another hymn. They must be nearing the end of the service. I looked around for escape. It wouldn't do to be caught red-eyed when the mourners came out.

Across the lawn and on the other side of the street was the parking lot, crammed with empty automobiles. A group of chauffeurs clustered in one corner, chatting in properly lowered voices. The cars were empty, all save one in which two men were talking together in the back. I thought I recognized Sidney Muss.

Then I saw Roberts, Aunt Lydie's chauffeur, leaning on the hood of her car and giving me a half wave of greeting. He opened the door and waved me toward it, offering refuge. I went.

"Thank you, Roberts. I'll just sit here a minute. I made a fool of myself in there."

"Funerals are no fun, Mrs. Willum. Miss Wentworth didn't want to come, but she's here from Paris just the same."

I hadn't seen Aunt Lydie in the church, but it didn't surprise me that she had come. Her code of behavior was of her own making, and she stuck to it rigidly. Friendship and loyalty were high on her priority list, and Eleanore de Pauw had been a friend—not a close one but a friend nonetheless. There was no question but that she would fly back from Paris for this funeral, much as she hated anything to do with illness or death.

"When did she get in?" I asked. "She didn't call me."

"Last night, but Hannah said she was very tired. I know she's planning to see you this afternoon. She's ordered the Gainsborough Brown birthday present out of storage."

So, she had remembered!

The singing swelled, coming thinly and then more strongly through the now-open church doors. They were bringing Eleanore out, steps hesitating to the measured cadence of the music. Roberts had drawn himself up and was standing at respectful attention. Then the mourners were in the doorway, blinking in the sunlight; they began to straggle uncertainly down the walk. I saw Miss Ives among them; and my aunt, leaning on Gregor's arm. His head was bent down to her and he was talking furiously. Her eyes were downcast; she gave no sign that she was listening.

I noticed one of the drivers detach himself from the cluster of chauffeurs and step into the car with Muss in it.

I addressed Roberts's back, which was turned to me, stiff as a grenadier's. "I wonder why Mr. Muss didn't go inside the church."

Roberts allowed himself a twitch of the right shoulder. "Mr. Muss's car has been there the whole time, ever since we got here. I don't think he ever intended to go in."

I twisted in my seat. From where I sat I could study the two men. One of them was Sidney Muss, all right. I couldn't tell about the other. His back was to me.

"He didn't go to the services? How odd!"

"Pulled in there. Parked. A man comes along and gets in with him. Been talking ever since. More like a board meeting than a funeral. Stay where you are, Mrs. Willum. I'll pick up Miss Wentworth and we'll drop you at your car. Just tell me where you're parked."

The hearse was moving off. The mourners had reached the street. Gregor was still talking to my aunt.

A car door slammed. The passenger had stepped out of Sidney Muss's car, which promptly leapt into gear and disappeared around the corner.

I had a good enough look at the man's face before he lost

himself among the cars of the parking lot. It was enough. I knew him. He was the man who had followed me the day I went to see Miss Ives in Briarcliff Manor. The same man I saw reflected in Gregor's mirror.

19

Ever since I was a little girl, I had had a fantasy about the people in the paintings on the walls of my aunt's library. It was the room in her house that Aunt Lydie used most; and when I was small, I used to wait there while she dressed to take me out. My fantasy was that the people in the pictures were real and that I could talk to them and they would understand, although they never answered. The Goya, the Rembrandt, the Memling, the Vermeer, the Hals . . . what secrets I had told them in the past! And how well they had kept them.

And here we all were again. I had come to pick up the sculpture. The butler had said my aunt would be back in a minute—she was riding—and meanwhile, wouldn't I like a cup of tea or a drink? I answered no, thank you, nothing now. And then I was alone with my old friends, who were gazing down at me with what I fancied was remembered affection.

"Dear friends," I began, "today I have only big secrets, so big that I hope you will forgive me if I don't tell them even to you." If Jennings, the butler, had come in just then, he would surely have thought me mad. But he didn't come in, Aunt Lydie did. And she wasn't even surprised. She stood in the doorway in her dove-grey riding clothes, gleaming boots and silver hair, a flotilla of small dogs bobbing about at her feet, and said, "Persis, I do believe you'll never grow up!"

"Not if I can help it," I replied, turning pink.

She laughed, and several of the dogs barked in accompaniment.

Jennings and two parlor maids arrived at this point with a tea table, which gleamed with silver and groaned under a burden of a dozen or so dishes. The three bustled about arranging things under my aunt's direction, and presently, when she was satisfied and the dogs looked as if they would faint with expectation, the servants withdrew.

My aunt surveyed the delicacies with a greedy gleam. "Isn't it just glorious?" she exclaimed. "Help yourself. Those little cress sandwiches are lovely. And the anchovy paste! Oh, do try some of these scones! I love them. Rhubarb jam, cherry preserves, heavenly shortbread . . ."

"Aunt Lydie," I protested, "there's enough here for eight hundred hungry boys. You and I can't possibly do justice to it all."

But my aunt was busy distributing the treats, and I realized that a troop of miniature dogs could tuck in as well as a battalion of small boys—and as quickly.

Then, all of a sudden, in the middle of choreographing this canine gluttony, she was addressing me again in such an offhand way that even I, accustomed though I was to her idiosyncratic tempo, was almost caught off guard.

"Gregor had a perfectly good reason for missing my birthday party, you know, and I suppose I shall have to forgive him. Although I really don't approve of business as an excuse."

I popped a cookie into my mouth to hide my confusion. What was Gregor up to now?

She looked at me crossly. "He couldn't come to my party because he had to break into Gainsborough Brown's studio while everyone was at my house. Something to do with that awful Mr. Brown selling paintings on his own. Miss Ives almost caught him at it before he found anything, which he never did. Climbed in through a window, if you can stand it. He'd found some paintings in Paris and heard

163

rumors there were more here. He told me all about it this morning at the funeral. And he's in financial trouble; he's learned that Mr. Sidney Muss is trying to get financial control of World Galleries under cover of advancing money for the expansion plans. It seems Gregor's having trouble getting other capital, with his star artist dead."

She sighed and frowned and nibbled absently on a pastry and sipped her tea while the dogs continued to decimate the food. I thought, I was right. Gregor *had* been to the studio before. Then I thought about Gregor being in the country the night of the party and Muss trying to take over World Galleries. I wondered how it all tied together . . .

When the serving dishes were finally in ruins, Aunt Lydie shooed the dogs outside and rang for Jennings.

"Now," she announced when that was done, "I've told them to bring up the birthday present. You've never seen it, have you? I thought not. You would have warned me. Well, I think you ought to before we decide to let Gregor show it."

They were carrying it into the room, Jennings and a couple of yard men, cradling the sections in their arms and looking to Aunt Lydie for instructions. They didn't get any help from her. She shrugged her shoulders and looked mystified. "Put them down anywhere and then you can go," she murmured. "Mrs. Willum will know what to do."

It didn't take me long. I had the pieces on their stands in less than ten seconds.

What Gainsborough had done was to take three shiny aluminum tubes that varied in height and diameter, cap the tops, and shape the bottoms so they could be mounted separately on black wooden bases. That was it. Period.

"Could he really have thought I'd like this?" My aunt was aghast at the idea.

No. Even Gains must have known she'd find this work stultifying and would banish it on sight. But maybe he wanted it that way. . . .

I studied the three silver columns with quickening

interest. It must be so. He had deliberately created something she would detest, something she would immediately consign to the fortresslike storage rooms of The Crossing. But why?

I stepped forward and put my hand on the cool shaft of the first column. Three perfect tubes. Three perfect hiding places. Perfect for ... I tugged at the cap that topped it. Nothing. I tried twisting, ever so gently. This time the obedient cap responded slightly. More pressure. It turned and came off in my hand.

"I really thought you'd want to look, Persis, before ... What on earth are you doing?"

I had my hand inside the tube, fingers exploring. "Everybody's been looking for paintings of Gainsborough's, Aunt Lydie ... at my house ... at Alida's ... at the gallery. I just thought ..." There *was* something. I could feel it. I caught at its edges and slowly and carefully began to withdraw my hand.

"Persis, what is it?"

And then they were out of their hiding place—unstretched canvases, carefully arranged between sheets of wax paper. And on the canvases, paintings ... Gainsborough Brown's.

Aunt Lydie was beside me. She had grasped the situation at once. Together we emptied the other aluminum tubes of their secrets, spreading out the pictures one by one to look at them and then rolling them up carefully again in their waxed protection. There were seventeen in all.

"They're not bad," Lydia Wentworth stated, firmly giving credit where credit was due.

"They're great," I said, just as positively. Because they were, for Gainsborough Brown.

"They're not signed," my aunt continued conversationally, being careful as usual not to ask questions. Her sharp eyes had noted immediately that not one of the paintings had a signature. I ought to tell her something—

anything, I thought. After all, they were hidden inside her birthday present.

But she wasn't worrying about signatures. She was thinking far ahead. "Persis, you realize that this is a delicate situation. Very delicate, indeed. If they're documented, these pictures could represent about a million dollars."

"At least," I agreed. Provenance would be no problem. They were unquestionably Gainsborough Browns ... and of his best period. With the artist dead, there was no way of guessing how high they would go, even without signatures.

"Very well. Then since they're so valuable, it's imperative that they should be discovered properly—in full view of the world, as it were—so there won't be any questions. And with as little personal publicity for me as possible." She grimaced. "Really, that terrible young man. How could he do this to me?"

Jennings came softly into the room while she was speaking and handed me a telephone. "A call for you, Mrs. Willum. A Mr. Greenspan. He says it's very important."

"Go ahead," said Aunt Lydie. "Don't pay any attention to me. I shall be deep in thought. I can see that this situation will require the utmost tact."

Marvin Greenspan's voice was unnaturally shrill. His agitation was immediately apparent. "Can you come over to my hospital right away? I hate to bother you, but it's important. I called your house and your housekeeper said it was all right to call you there."

"What is it?"

"We have a friend of yours here."

I didn't have to ask who it was. "I'll be right over," I told him.

"Please hurry," Greenspan said. And he rang off, a good Samaritan in distress.

———————

Marvin Greenspan's hospital was smack up against one of the busiest highways on the South Shore, with scarcely enough room between it and the road for an ambulance to

166

park without having its bumper removed by the passing traffic. It looked more like a big office building than anything else.

I approached the switchboard in the lobby, asked for Mr. Marvin Greenspan, and was directed to the third floor. The switchboard operator was wearing so much mascara that it must have been an effort for her to blink.

The place didn't look at all like hospitals I was more familiar with. In some ways, it resembled a resort. For example, there were travel posters on all the walls and not one, but three gift shops along the corridor I took to reach the elevator. No one looked worried or sick or even hypochondriacal. Finally, however, I noticed a middle-aged woman in a walking cast as I stepped out on the third floor.

Greenspan was waiting for me in front of the nurses' station. His tie was unknotted and his hair looked as if someone had just run a magnet back and forth above the top of his head.

"You came!" He sounded surprised, and grateful. "Not asking a single question, you just came! And after I disturbed you at Miss Wentworth's." He breathed her name with reverence. "She didn't mind, did she?"

"My aunt's the busiest woman I know, Mr. Greenspan," I said. "She always has a million things to do. She didn't even ask where I was going. Is it Susan? Is she all right?"

He shepherded me along a corridor. "Could you see your way clear to call me Marvin? All this Mr. Greenspanning makes me nervous." He stopped in front of an unmarked door. There were keys in his hand, and he was fitting them in the lock. "This is where we keep the drugs. Only authorized personnel have the key. The drug scene today is very, very bad. You'd be surprised at the stories I could tell you. But some other time. For now, this is a good place to talk without anyone hearing us. And I should explain first."

We were in a room full of bottles. Known dangers, all of them; but known dangers didn't frighten me.

Marvin leaned against the door, fished around for a

cigar, got as far as producing matches and then discarded the whole idea. He was so nervous he put the cigar back in his trouser pocket along with the matches.

"I don't know how I got mixed up in this, but here I am." He took a large gulp of air. "I'm working late last night—in the city if you want to keep afloat you open up when it's convenient for the client, not when it's convenient for you. So I'm expecting this fellow. He's interested in a forty-thousand-dollar picture. I don't mind a forty-thousand-dollar wait." His expression brightened momentarily. Then he was serious again. "The client doesn't show, but the redheaded Susan Evans does."

In the evening—how had she managed? I felt an ache of foreboding in all my limbs.

"She comes staggering in the door with just a coat buttoned up over her and she can hardly walk. I think she's loaded, but only for an instant. I've seen enough cases of beatings around here to recognize one when I see it. And this was a real nasty one. Those . . . If you could see . . ." His face was changing as he talked, his kindly eyes blazing.

"But why? For Heaven's sake, tell me!"

He sighed. The machinations of Fate were just too much for him. "Our good friend Mr. Oliver Reynolds was on television last night—the network news, something about his art film. And those thugs Muss hires are watching and they tell Muss this is the guy Susan Evans went to see at my gallery. Muss, who hates Reynolds, goes berserk and orders them to pound on her until she tells why she went to meet Reynolds. The more she says it was about a commission for a rich guy from Cleveland, the wilder Muss gets. Finally she passes out and they all leave the room to soak their fists in brine or something." (This last was delivered with savage irony.)

"But how did she get to you?"

"A miracle. Came to and got out the back before they returned. Lucky, and brave." He was unlocking the door and turning out the light. When we were in the hall again, he straightened his tie and made brushing motions at his hair with both hands. Then he began walking purposefully down the corridor ahead of me, his body rolling on his sturdy legs like a dinghy in a choppy sea. "Muss will be looking for her. He'll think of this place eventually."

He was right. Muss—aroused—would think of everything. "A guard . . . could you get a guard?"

"I've got an extra security man here for the time being, and that will help some. But I can't keep her here. I've had to lie. I could be in trouble."

It was true. If he'd falsified records or failed to report her as an accident case, he and his whole hospital could be in real trouble. "What did you say on her chart?"

He paused, looking acutely embarrassed. "A bad fall due to alcoholism." There was a longer pause. Greenspan, the gentle soul, was suffering. "I'm afraid there's some medical evidence—we've begun basic treatment—the charts wouldn't be entirely untruthful." He turned away resolutely and tapped on the door to his right before he pushed it open. "Not that I blame her one bit. After the hell she's been through, she's entitled." We entered Susan's room, and he pulled the door shut behind us.

I never would have known her. They hadn't spared her face this time. There were stitches in her forehead. Both of her eyes were bruised and black. Her nose—her beautiful nose—had been broken. And there was something else . . .

"Broken jaw," Greenspan whispered. "Wired. Dislocated shoulder, too. Other things. A miracle she walked." He had gone directly to her bedside and was making soft, patting motions over one of the bloodless hands that lay limp on the sheet. He must have been one of those little boys who rescue fallen baby birds.

She was completely still; under sedation, I thought. Helpless.

"We have to get her out of here." I was whispering, too. "Muss will trace her to you."

"I could move her in an ambulance, but where? She will need care for a while."

"Mrs. Howard!" I exclaimed suddenly, then lowered my voice again. "Her niece has a rest home. The perfect place—and no tracks!" I explained rapidly, and Greenspan said it could be done. He would see to all the arrangements as soon as I gave him the word. I knew it was the right solution when I saw how pleased he was. Nothing but a perfect solution would have satisfied him. He even permitted himself a smile. His fallen bird would be safe. In an ecstasy of relief, he leaned over and began to fuss with the covers at her shoulder, his stubby hands gentle on the whiteness of the cotton.

"They won't hurt you again," he told her. "I won't let them do it."

She stirred a little, but her eyes remained closed.

"Something's going on with Sidney Muss," I said, as much to myself as to Greenspan. "That beating was for more than jealousy."

Greenspan nodded vigorously. "Agreed. He's afraid of something. I think they might have killed her eventually." Our eyes met and a chill went through both of us as we realized that we had been thinking the same thing. Susan Evans stirred again and moaned. This time her eyelids fluttered.

Muss played a more-than-rough game, and he played without rules. We had to fight back somehow, for her sake.

"Do you think she could answer one question?" I asked Greenspan.

"Maybe." He leaned over her once more, calling her name softly and insistently. While she struggled to respond, I got my sketchbook out of my bag and opened it to the drawing I had made of Muss's parking-lot companion, holding it ready for her to see when her eyes opened. Presently they did open, the pupils large and unfocused. I doubted if she was really aware of anything, but I had to try.

"Susan, I saw this man with Mr. Muss this morning. Do you know him? Did he have anything to do with what they did to you?"

"Don't try to speak, honey, just move your hand if it's 'yes,'" Greenspan said gently. "Do you know him?"

Her eyes still appeared unfocused to me. Was she really looking? I doubted it. But then she surprised me. Her hand moved. The answer was "yes."

"Did he have anything to do with what happened to you?" I waited, scarcely daring to breathe. I waited a long time. The hand never moved.

"Do you know his name?" Again the long wait; again no sign. Had she drifted away from us, back into that peaceful, silent, pain-free world to which only drugs held the key?

"I think that's it," Marvin Greenspan said, finally.

I closed my sketchbook and put it away, overwhelmed by the keenness of my disappointment. We had tried. All we could do now was take care of her. Perhaps later when she was better we could talk.

"I'll have all the arrangements made by tomorrow," I told him. "Call the rest home in the afternoon. Here's the name of my housekeeper's niece. I think you should use a pay phone, and I don't think you and I should talk again. We must be careful."

We had moved to the door and were making our final plans in the conspiratorial whispers we had used earlier when both of us heard a sound from the bed. Susan Evans was making a noise far back in her throat. She was trying to get our attention. She was trying to speak. We rushed back to her side.

She had to fight to deliver each word, working hard to overcome the double handicap of the drugs and an inflexibly wired jaw, fighting to master the pain and the lassitude and the confusion, determined to speak because, I suppose, I had been kind to her and I had asked a question to which she felt she owed an answer.

The words were blurred. There was an unconscionable wait between each one. But we could comprehend them perfectly.

171

What she said was, "Just . . . a foreigner . . . doing art research . . . Muss . . . summer place . . . this . . . fall."

That was all.

20

During the next few days, I found it increasingly difficult to concentrate on everyday things. Part of the reason was the late hours I was keeping, painting until far into the night. But that was the smallest part.

Mrs. Howard noticed. "What's the matter with you, Mrs. Willum? You look awful. My niece says that girl's doing well. So what's wrong? You act like the world's coming to an end."

Well, maybe it was—my world, anyway. Maybe that was just the trouble. I'd started out, half-seriously, asking myself questions about Gainsborough Brown's death, an event that was over and done with. And suddenly it wasn't over and done with at all, quite the contrary. The maze of events, culminating in the death of Eleanore de Pauw and the attack on Susan, was making me claustrophobic. Culminating? No, that was exactly what disturbed me. I had a clammy feeling that there was more to come.

At least one other person felt the unease that was affecting me, and that was Oliver Reynolds. He turned up unannounced one day, and I was surprised to see that he looked every bit as haggard as I did. In fact, it would have been hard to decide which of us had the bigger circles under his eyes.

"I've brought you a gun," he said without preamble, "and I want you to keep it with you every minute."

Nothing could have startled me more. "Oliver, you're mad! What do I want with a gun? I've never touched one in my life." I didn't say, if you think I'm a mental case why give me a gun? But that's what I thought.

He glared at me from bloodshot eyes. "Well, you're going to touch one now. There it is. Take it. This is how it works. The main thing to remember is that there are six shells." He pushed the thing into my hand. "This is the hammer . . . the frame . . . the barrel . . . the butt. This is the trigger, but you must know that. Look, you flip this and it opens the cylinder. Here's an extra box of shells. You drop the shells in. The cylinder revolves when the hammer goes back, placing the next shell in line with the barrel. You line up your sights on your target. This is a Colt thirty-eight, sufficient at close range to make quite a large, ventilating gap in a body."

I saw the small, round medallion with the running horse on it that identified the gun as a Colt; it was the only pretty thing about it. "Why are you doing this?" I asked with distaste.

He didn't relent. "I want you to promise you'll keep it with you, even next to your bed at night. Now, promise."

But I was digging in, surprised at my own stubbornness. Once I had wanted him to listen to me about Gainsborough's murder, and he wouldn't. Now he wanted me to keep a gun, and I wouldn't. "No. I'm not a scared baby."

His voice crackled with exasperation. "Would I offer a gun to a scared baby? Don't you see, Persis, I believe you? God knows I owe you an apology for not believing you from the beginning, but at least I believe you now. That's why I'm here."

Well! It was nice of him. Yes. And I was more than pleasantly surprised, if one could say there was anything pleasantly surprising in a matter involving murder. But the switch was too sudden, too unexpected to be grasped all at once. First the gun, now this! Oliver the cautious and stodgy. If it had been Aunt Lydie doing an about-face, or Gregor, who was almost as unpredictable . . .

"Why did you change your mind?" I even sounded suspicious to myself.

"It was Eleanore de Pauw. I don't think it was an accident. I got to brooding about it, Persis. And you know something? She never would have gone rushing off to that place, Oak Hill, in the middle of a bad storm because I remember that she wasn't very fond of driving." He was in dead earnest, his seriousness so intense that it made a mockery of his usual pleasant expression. "Only one thing would make her go."

"One thing?" I had an idea of what that one thing would be, but I wanted to hear him say it.

"A phone call saying that Dickie was at Oak Hill with a girl—a good-looking young girl, like the one Dickie was with at Lydia's party. That would get her out fast."

He was quite right. Oak Hill would have been the perfect place for a rendezvous. We didn't speak for a moment, each of us sadly imagining the telephone call and the anonymous voice ("This is a friend calling") warning Eleanore. Then her frantic rush to the car, the wild drive.

"Of course," Oliver said, "she couldn't have missed the sign, no matter how bad conditions were. Unless it was invisible."

"I know."

"So I drove there last night, hung my coat over it, piled some branches in front and came back down the road again. There was no moon."

I'd thought of this, too. "And?"

He let out a long breath. "It was invisible."

There it was. He'd reasoned it out exactly as I had done, reaching the same conclusions. It seemed that I had an ally at last.

"You see now why I want you to have a gun. Nothing must happen to you, Persis. You haven't spoken to anyone else about this, have you?"

I shook my head. "No one."

He was relieved. "Good. Don't. And keep the gun handy."

He knew perfectly well I'd never use it, but I nodded anyway. There was no point in arguing.

Afterward I wondered why he hadn't suggested that we go to the police. Surely, with him to back me up, they would listen to my contention that two people had been murdered. Or would they? The truth of the matter was that we still had no proof.

———

I carried that gun around with me for just about three hours, that's all. Either it weighed a ton or it just felt that way. After a hundred and eighty extremely uncomfortable minutes, I rationalized that since I was never going to fire the weapon anyway, there was no point in lugging it about. My feelings of apprehension were bad enough without the gun as a reminder. So I put it in my desk drawer and tried to forget about it.

I don't know why my apprehension kept growing. Reports on Susan Evans were good; there hadn't been a sound out of Sidney Muss; Gregor was being unusually pleasant; and my aunt kept me busy discussing a new plan each day for how to orchestrate the public discovery of the Gainsborough Brown paintings. (I think she was secretly enjoying it.)

But when the call came from Gregor, I wasn't surprised. I had been expecting something, if not a culmination, then certainly something that would mark a turning point in this affair. There is always a third thing. The death of Gainsborough, then Eleanore's "accident." Number three was still a question mark, but I was afraid it might be Alida.

Gregor was calling from her house. His plummy voice was slightly off-key, like a piano slipping out of tune. "Could you do me a very big favor, Persis? Could you put Alida up at your house until my dinner party Friday?"

"You know I will, but why?" I wasn't like Aunt Lydie. I asked questions.

The voice slid another half note. "She's just tried to kill herself, and you know how suicides are—they always try again. You and Mrs. Howard have got to keep an eye on her. I need her Friday night."

Dear God but he sounded callous. He needed her for Friday night when she'd just tried to commit suicide. Was that all he could think of? He couldn't mean it the way it sounded. That was just Gregor, all wrapped up in his business affairs. Friday night was when he was going to unveil Gainsborough's birthday present to Aunt Lydie. Naturally he would want to be sure Alida was present.

"Keep her in bed. She's weak. So am I, for that matter," he said.

"What did she do?"

"Pills. In her iced tea." His emotions got the better of him for a moment. "Christ, we were lucky, Persis! I just walked in and found her, and Maggie came not too long after. Alida had sent her down to the village on an errand. Between us, we got her cleaned out and on her feet, finally. Imagine if I hadn't stopped by and Maggie had called a doctor!"

"What do you mean, Gregor? Haven't you called a doctor?"

"And have it all over the newspapers?" He was beside himself at the mere idea. "She's pretending she didn't mean to take those pills. They always do that." He talked as if he'd had experience with this kind of thing before. No doubt he had. Among all his female acquaintances there could easily have been a few hysterical pill-takers. Well, at least he had known what to do in the circumstances; that was a blessing. "Just a minute. Maggie's here and she's saying something."

He put the telephone down, and I could hear the sounds of their conversation, although the words were indecipherable. In that interim, I called to Mrs. Howard and asked her to get the guest room ready for Alida. Her burst of enthusiasm at having a visitor in the house carried her up the stairs on the double, humming with anticipation.

"Persis? Sorry. Maggie is upset." Gregor was back. "I've sent her upstairs to Alida again. In fact, Maggie's damn

177

near hysterical. She's got a fixation that we'll blame this on her because Alida got her hands on those pills after you said to hide them. And she's having a fit because I found the front door open when I came. Claims she locked it and won't admit that she must have forgotten. Damn lucky that it was open, of course. I'm ordering her to go home for a couple of days, and that has really set her off. She thinks I don't trust her to look after Alida. Honestly, women!" Gregor was out of patience; he'd had it for one day. I didn't blame him. If the saving of Alida Brown's life had entailed the kind of unromantic messiness I imagined, he would be truly fed up. "God, Persis, what a fool thing for her to do! And now, of all times!"

"I'd hoped she was coming out of it," I said sadly. "She was beginning to take an interest in things. She'd assured me she was turning over a new leaf."

"Well, don't trust her," he warned. "She'll try it again for sure, if we let her. They always do," he repeated. Then he told me that Maggie was packing for Alida and that he'd be along with our new guest in about half an hour.

I went outside and wandered around in the garden looking for something still blooming to put in the guest room. There wasn't much that was inspiring—fall was making its first inroads. Everything that remained flaunted the colors that lacked tranquility—garish golds and oranges and reds—beautiful together but too vibrant and full of life for someone who had tried to take her own.

If she had tried to take her own.

"She pretended she didn't mean to take those pills," Gregor had said.

Maggie insisted she'd locked the front door.

Suppose both of them were right. Suppose Alida had let someone in the house. . . .

I moved absentmindedly about in the cutting garden, carelessly snipping and mixing the last of the zinnias and the few remaining nasturtiums. It was conceivable that Alida might want to take her own life, I was thinking. She had certainly been depressed enough. On the other hand, there was the balcony railing that had so conveniently given way.

When I finally came back inside, I was surprised to find that I had gathered a very pretty bouquet—very pretty indeed. Much prettier than the thoughts that had been distracting me.

———————

She hadn't wanted to come, poor thing. It was obvious in every faltering step as she came up the walk, leaning heavily on Gregor's arm. I could tell that she wanted more than anything to be back in the sanctuary of her safe house, with its locked windows and bolted doors, safe in her own cocoon. She didn't say anything, but the message was plain.

On the other hand, since she was here, she appeared to have made up her mind to make the best of it; and from the moment Gregor left her with Mrs. Howard and me, she made a real effort to be cooperative, no doubt hoping that the more willingly she took the vitamins Gregor had ordered, the sooner she would be well enough to leave us. She came as close to being the perfect guest as anyone possibly could—docile and quiet and unobtrusive. By the end of the second day, I was sure that another forty-eight hours would find her perfectly able to attend Gregor's dinner. In other words, we would make it just in time. And she seemed willing to go, maybe to make up to him for the trouble she'd caused, maybe because going would mean she was also well enough to go home.

I couldn't understand why she'd want to return to that big house unless it was the same instinct that drives the horse back to his burning stall. She never said a word about her supposed suicide attempt, although I did my best to draw her out. As her response to my every gentle effort was to remain silent or change the subject, I soon gave it up. I suppose Gregor would have labeled her reticence typical of the self-destructive personality cannily planning a next attempt, but I couldn't agree.

She smiled a lot, for her—sad smiles. And she read or

looked out the window into the garden. We didn't urge her to sit outside. There was already a chill in the air. The only time she caused any trouble was the night I woke up and found she wasn't in her bed. Even that was nothing. I discovered her downstairs with all the lights on, staring at my old Gainsborough Browns. It was odd, but she appeared to be studying the signatures.

She seemed to look forward to her afternoon chats with Mrs. Howard, who had taken to her at once because they shared a passion for tea . . . Mrs. Howard believed that all tea-drinkers were superior to all non-tea-drinkers, even if they happened to prefer it long and tall and iced, as Alida did. Actually, the afternoon chats were one-sided, meaning that Mrs. Howard carried on a spirited monologue about the latest deaths and illnesses in the village, interspersed with tirades of complaint against Blackstone.

They were upstairs in the middle of one of these tête-à-têtes when I returned home from work early, just to make sure Alida was all right. I'd left too soon that morning for the 10 A.M. mail. It was waiting for me now on the hall table, and the first thing I saw was a special delivery letter from an M. Green. It didn't ring any bells.

Upon tearing it open, I realized that it was from Greenspan, whose caution was colored by his taste for fictional intrigue. He had typed the letter himself, X-ing out words with a cheerful abandon that gave the whole thing the flavor of his own pell-mell speech.

> Dear Mrs. Willum,
>
> Rumors are flying downtown. First, I hear you have an important guest staying with you and I hope she's behaving.
>
> [Poor Alida! How quickly things got around, in spite of every effort. So they were gossiping already about her suicide attempt.]
>
> There's another rumor going around I think you should XXXXXX know about. XXX The boys on my street are saying a certain XXXX man—we both

know him, so you can guess who—never got rid of his first bum cargo and is planning to have changes made and unload it abroad, where buyers aren't so critical.

Our other project XXX flourishes.

All the best
M. Green

Greenspan certainly had a talent for being cryptic. "Our other project"—Susan Evans. I already was aware of her progress, as Mrs. Howard gave me the news every day.

"A man—we both know him"—that was more interesting. The only man we both knew who had a first "bum cargo" was The Collector, with his first collection of fakes. Sidney Muss, who was maneuvering to get control of World Galleries.

21

It's really funny how some small thing will put you on the track of something perfectly obvious—something you ought to have recognized long ago.

It was that way about Miss Ives. The small click must have occurred when I found Alida Brown studying the signatures of those three Gainsborough Browns of mine. All of a sudden a bigger light turned on in my head, and I went to see Hope Ives the very next morning in the apartment above Gains's studio. Her belongings were almost completely packed.

"I'm leaving as soon as Mr. Olitsky's dinner party is over," she told me. "I'm going to go back to Briarcliff Manor to teach school."

She was wearing her mousy personality: dress too big, shoes too wide, glasses too thick. She was carefully folding up sheets and towels, and putting them in a cardboard carton.

"I think it's a good idea," I said, sitting down on the only chair that didn't have something already on it. "I would certainly think you ought to get away from here before somebody else figures out that you are really Gainsborough Brown."

She made the funniest sound.

"I think I have most of it figured out—stop me if I make a mistake." Her hands went on automatically making folding motions with the towel she was holding, but she stared right through me. It was eerie.

"When Gains went to New York and disappeared that first time, it was your work he took with him, wasn't it? Your paintings, which he said were his own. And when you finally caught up with him, you let him go on passing your work off as his own for fear of losing him."

She didn't say a word. But she didn't deny it, either.

"You thought anything was worth it as long as you kept him. So you painted your heart out, and he took the credit."

I wondered if the act of painting itself hadn't become an agony under those conditions. And imagine how she must have felt when he asked for a divorce!

"You must have had the good sense to be uneasy when he wanted to divorce you. Right? I suppose he actually had the gall to ask you to go on painting for him after the divorce as a purely business arrangement?" She nodded. "He would," I said bitterly.

She was extremely pale. "I knew all along he would leave me the minute he found someone with enough money. That's all he really cared for—money. Not art. Just money, so he could move with his 'high life,' as he said."

"And I'll bet he never actually gave you a penny of all the money you earned?" Her expression said that I was right again. "So you decided to paint yourself some 'insurance.'"

She looked like a dog that expected to be beaten, and I knew I was right.

"You couldn't let him know what you were doing, so you had to paint at night, while he slept. Painting all night under artificial light for yourself and then painting all day for him. A hideous routine." As a painter, I would know.

"My eyes . . ." It was involuntary.

"I can imagine. No one could have stood it. Headaches. Blurring. Vision going from bad to worse. And you, painting in simpler and simpler forms, finally, because you could scarcely see. It must have been awful."

"I thought I was going blind; I *was* going blind. And I

183

didn't dare let anyone know. I kept thinking about all the great artists who had gone blind, or nearly so. Pissarro, Degas, Monet . . ."

"Daumier, Pierro della Francesca . . ." I think I was accurate.

"I know. And I'd think about Renoir, at the end, painting with his brushes strapped to his arthritic hands. And Matisse only able to do paper cut-outs, finally. And I couldn't feel sorry for myself at all. Anyway, I struggled and managed to finish twenty . . ." she stopped.

"Twenty 'insurance' paintings—twenty real beauties that would see you through in case Gains ever really left you for good." I was excited now. "Twenty pictures that rivaled anything you'd ever done in the past."

She wasn't denying anything. "They were good." It was said simply, a statement of fact.

"And you didn't sign them. So if Gains somehow got his hands on them, he could never fully benefit from them. And he did get his hands on them, didn't he? How else could three unsigned Gainsborough Browns have turned up in Europe? He discovered them one night when he was trying to give someone a poster. You had done the classic trick of hiding them right under his nose in the backs of the framed posters in his studio! You had no reason to suppose he would ever be tampering with those posters."

"I never knew what he did with them after he found them."

"I think I have an idea. I think he looked over my garage with an idea of hiding them there. But if he did hide them there, it could only have been for a very brief time. He had a better place in mind. And, in the meantime, he sold three in Paris." No point in mentioning that he sold them to finance his courtship of Alida and to buy the false papers that elevated Aunt Lydie to the sacred state of mother-hood.

"Yes, but where?"

I had no intention of telling her where. Let her wait with everyone else until tomorrow night at Gregor's.

"But how did you find out? First about my being his wife and now this? I thought I was safe."

"You were clever, all right. But to begin with, I never understood how Gains painted those pictures. Especially in the beginning. They were too sensitive to fit his personality. Oh, I know it doesn't mean anything. Artists aren't necessarily anything like their work. I kept telling myself that over and over, but I was never convinced. Then there was your note—remember? The one where you sent me the studio key. I'd never seen your handwriting before. Did you realize that? Always only your scribbled hieroglyphics. You slipped up and had the actual words 'Gainsborough Brown' in the note. Something stuck in my mind at the time but subliminally. Then, when I saw Alida actually studying the signatures on the Gainsborough Browns at my house, I took a hard look at the signatures myself—I hadn't *really* looked at his signature for years—to see what was so interesting. And it seemed to me I'd seen something like that lately . . . in your letter, that's where."

"Artist's eye," she murmured. It was true. Again.

"And your glasses," I continued. "Why make such a point of having me look through them when I found you in Briarcliff? Why make such a point of proving to me that you didn't need glasses unless the opposite was true? I got to thinking about all those things and I put them all together, especially when I finally located your doctor—the one who's so cross with you because you never filled his prescriptions until after Gains died."

"He'd have left me."

"Gains, you mean? But you're almost blind."

"He was fussy about women's looks, you know that. He'd have left me." There wasn't any doubt in her mind. "When we were alone I always had to dress up." I think she was actually a little proud of it. "And if he ever knew I couldn't see—and couldn't paint—"

"I thought of that. I suppose you wouldn't have dared take the risk of letting him know anything." It was all such a waste for you, Ives, I thought. He'd have left you anyway, sooner or later, eyes or no eyes.

"There was one last thing. Gains would never have sold a painting without the signature because he could get so much more for it signed. So I had to think that maybe it *wasn't* his signature, and, inescapably, maybe *he* wasn't the artist. By the way, what happened when he discovered your 'insurance' paintings?"

"I knew he found them the day I walked into the studio and saw that the posters were gone. I didn't say anything. I couldn't. I knew it was all over for me, but I didn't say anything because I didn't want to give up."

So she had stayed on, hoping for God knows what. "You were certainly a good painter, Miss Ives." It was my tribute.

"Thank you, Mrs. Willum. But I wasn't really," she said. "I couldn't do anything but landscape, you know. That was what I loved. I had a feeling for it. Figures, no, I was awful. But Gains knew what the public wanted and he made me paint them. Truly, Mrs. Willum, he was more responsible than I was for the success of my work. I'm fully aware of that. I always have been."

I couldn't believe it. She was still defending him.

"And, Mrs. Willum?"

"Yes?"

"You know I didn't do the things in his studio this last time. You know I didn't sign them either. I only signed the work I did myself."

"I know. Gains signed those. That's why the signatures were so different. He was delighted with himself, I'm sure, to have got a show together without your help. I can just imagine how he gloated! But the 'insurance' paintings—did you try to find them?"

"Of course. I looked all through Alida's house. I suppose the rest of them will turn up someday, somewhere . . ."

I thought about my part in having arranged for them to "turn up." I sympathized with Miss Ives—such a tragedy for any artist to lose his eyes. But she had been determined to hold on to that brute despite the cost. I also thought

186

about my playing at detective. Could anyone who painted
with her sensitivity possibly be a killer?

At Gregor's, we were sixteen for dinner—eight people
from the world of museums and the media, and eight who
were connected to *l'affaire* Gainsborough: Alida Brown,
coming out of seclusion for the first time; Lydia Wentworth, breaking two of her most inflexible rules in a single
night by knowingly exposing herself to the press and
allowing something from her collection to leave The
Crossing; Oliver Reynolds; Miss Ives; me; and Dickie de
Pauw, whose claim to fame was that he had discovered the
body. Also, Sidney Muss.

We were bait, all of us, and pretty juicy bait at that. It
was obvious that we were there to drum up interest not
only in the immediate prospect of the public unveiling of
Gainsborough's first sculpture, but in the show of his last
works, whenever Gregor decided to unleash that set of
horrors on the public.

No sooner had Alida and I set foot in Gregor's living
room than Dickie blared, "Don't exactly know what I'm
doing here. Olitsky told me the Old Girl would have
wanted me to come. Good deed for you, Alida, you poor
little thing. Didn't tell me these newspaper fellas would be
here, though. Don't know how the Old Girl would take
that."

Alida paled, and Gregor and I exchanged worried
glances. Both of us were petrified that Dickie might have
heard about Alida's suicide attempt and would blurt that
out next. I moved as fast as I could, but not before Dickie
almost put his foot in it again. "You look awful, Alida," he
was beginning, and then I was upon him and giving him
such a friendly kiss that he forgot whatever he was going to
say.

Things went better after that. Aunt Lydie made her
entrance in a swirl of floating pink chiffon, wearing the
famous Wentworth diamond and ruby necklace designed
for her grandmother with each perfect ruby carved in the

shape of a leaf. The fact that she appeared in it was worth a paragraph in any paper. It had been a famous piece of jewelry for over a hundred years.

The press and museum people didn't quite step on each other in their scramble to get next to her and talk to her, but there were some rumpled ties and smudged makeup.

Gregor was busy explaining that she had brought the late Gainsborough Brown's gift with her in its original carton; and that her chauffeur was even now setting it up on the veranda, where we would all—Gregor included—see it for the first time after dinner.

That was how my aunt had finally decided to do it. The paintings would be discovered right here in front of all these people. It was, as she said to me, "next door to honest," and while there would be a sensation over it for a day or so, it would at least be a sensation involving fifteen people in addition to Lydia Wentworth. It was to be my job to "discover" the paintings when the moment came. She would be merely one of the surprised spectators. Knowing it would be impossible to dissuade her, I approved the scheme.

Gregor had ordered the drinks to be mixed on the generous side, and they took effect rather quickly, I thought. Even Miss Ives, in a moldy green dress, seemed to be loosening up, and Alida was looking less like a hot-house flower.

If there was animosity between the two of them, no one could have spotted it. The same was true of Sidney Muss. He gave no sign, standing next to Oliver Reynolds, that the sight of the former art critic on television had panicked him into ordering a savage beating for Susan Evans. Quite the contrary. He was as poised and self-satisfied in his too-expensive clothes as a cat who had caught and eaten a cock pheasant. Our communication was limited to a frigid nod. It was clear that since I had bumbled into his studio and discovered Susan Evans, he'd closed his books on me. By that one act I had learned too much about him.

In a way it was like a stage inhabited by a troupe of mad

mummers because all of us were play-acting, really. I couldn't believe some of the things I heard myself saying, and I'm sure I wasn't the only one. At one point Dickie de Pauw gave a long speech about how you could tell Gainsborough Brown was a genius merely by looking into his eyes. He didn't even know Gains, actually. The closest he could have come to looking into his eyes was after he was dead. I wondered if the eight people we had been brought here to impress sensed that we were making a mockery of the truth with our performances.

At exactly the right psychological moment, dinner was announced. The dining room resembled a funeral parlor, with an extravagant display of flowers and dripping candles. But the excellence of Gregor's food and the wines kept the atmosphere from being funereal.

Gregor made sure he spiced the meal with drama. During the fourth course, he had a few chosen words for me. Inasmuch as I was at the far end of the table from him, no one could possibly have missed what he had to say. "Persis, my dear, you must rescue me. The big man at the Tate is flying in from London especially to discuss Gai . . . well, to discuss something really big. I'll have to be in town with him for several days, ironing out details. So will you take charge in the interim?"

Every head at the table turned, including those of the two powerful curators who were flanking me. Which was exactly as Gregor had intended, obviously.

During the sixth course, he tapped on his wine glass and stood up. "Ladies and gentlemen, I have an announcement to make."

He waited for all conversation to die down before he continued. I was sure he was going to announce his engagement to my aunt. I don't know why; I just was.

But no. "I give you my new partner in World Galleries . . . one of the greatest patrons of the arts, whose impeccable taste has built one of the world's most superb private collections. My new partner—Lydia Wentworth!"

There was a collective gasp . . . a moment of dead silence

. . . a tentative spate of applause . . . and finally a vigorous burst of hand clapping and "Hear! Hear!" when the full impact of the announcement had been absorbed. I couldn't resist a quick glance at Sidney Muss. He was ashen. He seemed barely able to rise in time to join the rest of us, who had now stood to toast Aunt Lydie and Gregor and the success of their partnership.

I had taken the fact that she was wearing the famous Wentworth necklace as proof that she still cared enough for Gregor to want to please him by being more than ordinarily elegant for his party. Now I knew it was more than that. It was proof that when she went into business she went all the way, with all flags—and diamonds—flying. And I wondered whether it was love or the fact that Muss was maneuvering to get control of Gregor's galleries that had made her decide to back Gregor.

The elaborate meal finally came to an end, and Gregor urged us all toward the veranda with a graceful little speech about Gainsborough's birthday present to Lydia Wentworth. Sixteen people rose and moved outside, where Gainsborough's three aluminum tubes gleamed dramatically in the spotlights Gregor had had installed.

It was time. I squeezed up close and put my hand on the first of the shining cylinders. "So beautifully pure. So tranquil. So effective. A truly moving statement," I said, making sure that my voice carried. "And something else. All of us museum and gallery people who are forever bedeviled by shipping and insurance problems will appreciate this. See how easily the work can be dismantled and moved!"

There was a polite murmur of appreciation. I gave the cap of the first tube a quick twist. This was where I was going to put my hand inside and discover Miss Ives's last Gainsboroughs.

Only I didn't. Not in the first. Not in the second. Not in the third.

The paintings were gone.

22

All the next day I brooded. Gregor might as well have sent a deaf-mute to take care of everything. All I could think about was Gainsborough Brown . . . the missing paintings . . . Eleanore de Pauw . . . Susan Evans . . . the whole mess. I went round and round and over and over it all in my mind, chain smoking, and even, at one point, considering a trip to the closet where Mrs. W. kept her bottle. That's how desperate I was. And all I got for my pains was a monumental headache brought on by thinking in circles.

Finally I told myself that I would have to stop thinking about the whole picture and try to concentrate on just one aspect of it if I was going to get anywhere. That's what an old professor of mine at the Art Students' League used to tell me. "Focus, Persis," he would say. It's the only thing I do remember him saying.

I decided to focus on last night.

Who could have taken the paintings from inside those aluminum tubes when only my aunt and I and a dead man knew they were there?

There were two possibilities. Either someone else *did* know they were there and hadn't been able to get at them while they were safely stored at Aunt Lydie's; or someone who knew the paintings existed had been smart enough to figure out by a process of elimination that they might be hidden in the sculptures. Both seemed highly unlikely.

Still, Gregor had rushed around before dinner last night broadcasting to everyone that Roberts was setting up the birthday present on the veranda.

But nobody had left the dinner party. And Roberts had been with the aluminum tubes and had been told to *stay* with them.

Unless someone slipped into another room to make a quick phone call while we were at cocktails. Who would have noticed? And unless Roberts had gone into the kitchen for a bit of refreshment while we were all safely seated at dinner.

It could be . . . it could have worked that way. Somebody with nerve and the willingness to act quickly. Somebody with an accomplice? Sidney Muss? Was it possible he also knew about the missing paintings? With Sidney Muss anything was possible. And he was the one man who could summon minions into action on short notice.

I waited until I got home to telephone Marvin Greenspan. It was just a precaution. I didn't want anyone at the gallery to overhear. "Didn't Susan say something about Muss having a summer place that night we saw her in the hospital?" I asked.

"That's right, she did."

"Do you suppose she knows where it is? Did she ever mention it to you? It could be anywhere. I don't find him listed on Long Island. But that doesn't mean anything—he would probably have an unlisted number anyway."

Greenspan agreed. "Could be anywhere. I'll ask Susan. I think she'd tell me if she knew. She trusts me. And if she doesn't know I'll try Vic Longmaier. He's got big ears and he's in and out of Muss's New York studio all the time. He may have heard something. I'll get back to you."

"Right away?"

"Sure. But what's your hurry? You're not going to do anything dumb like go there, I hope. Because if you are, forget it. I'm not going to tell you anything. One beat-up woman is enough for me."

"Of course I'm not going to do anything stupid. Why

would I? I'm just curious, that's all. I've got an overactive curiosity gland."

"It killed a cat, honey." But I knew he'd find out for me. He was too nice ever to refuse a lady anything.

It was at Mill Point, on the water. He must have had it built to his own specifications, because it looked more like a cement bunker than anything. Just the sort of thing he'd go for, I thought. It glimmered whitely at me in the dusk, looking out of place in the pastoral North Shore landscape. Come to think of it, Muss would have looked out of place in this setting, too. He may have designed his house as an act of defiance.

A light mist was coming in from the Sound, and I supposed that it would turn into a true fog a little later. I had pulled my car over among the trees, back where the long driveway began, and had come the rest of the way on foot—no point in announcing myself with a brass band. The place no doubt had a superintendent living somewhere on the grounds; but chances were his house wouldn't be too close to the main house, and if I didn't advertise my arrival he might never know I was there. The main house, I knew, would be sure to be empty. Greenspan had reported that according to Susan Evans, Muss was never in residence—not even overnight—at this time of year. He would divide his time and his staff between New York and Palm Beach until next summer.

I stood for a few minutes next to the juniper hedge that bordered the entrance courtyard, wondering if, by some chance, there could be a watchman inside. While I stood there, lights blazed on suddenly and simultaneously in strategic rooms all over the house. I almost lost my nerve and ran. Then I realized that they must all be on an automatic timer to discourage burglars and vandals.

My next concern was for a burglar alarm. Surely this house would be wired to the hilt. There are two kinds of alarms in use in our area: One type sets off a terrible racket that would alert anyone within some distance; the other kind feeds directly into the local police headquarters with a taped voice message of a robbery in progress. Beside the front door I spotted the lighted button that signified that one of these systems was on and in working order. However much Muss ordinarily relied on the protection of the hoodlums that formed his everyday guard of honor, it was obvious that he counted on the same old safety measures as the rest of us when he left his house empty.

I began to circle cautiously around the house, taking care to stay out of the fingers of light that reached out here and there for a short span before dissolving in the mists. Suddenly I noticed a building off to the right. It was separated from the view of the big white bunker by a rigidly pruned yew hedge; and it looked like a renovated greenhouse. All the glass seemed to have been left in place on the side facing the water. The north side—it would have to be the north side—this was the North Shore of Long Island, wasn't it?

A studio. It had to be. North light.

I moved quickly toward it, not bothering to be too quiet. No one would hear me over the water noises on the beach not more than fifty yards away. There was a light inside, but not like the 100-watt ones in the big house. This was different. I stopped when I got near the door and listened. It seemed to me that I stood there for a very long time. All I heard was the multiple busy sounds of the waves.

I could see no alarm button burning here. So finally, after what seemed like a million years of standing without moving a muscle, I did what I had come to do and stepped forward and tried the door. After a brief instant of resistance it opened.

The part of the greenhouse I stood in had been made into living quarters. A quick glance showed me a kitchen unit dead ahead and what I made out to be a bedroom to the right. What light there was came from the left and I followed it into a long, mostly unfurnished room, unless you could call paintings furniture. For there were canvases everywhere—on the floor, on the window sill of the north wall, stacked all around the edges of the room. And there was something else . . . smells. Smells of paint and varnishes and turpentine. There was no mistaking the scent of artists' tools. This room was being used right now as a workroom.

The lure of the canvases drew me into the room. A whole room full of paintings never hurt anyone, pictures were safe enough. And they were what I had come for.

But what strange pictures they were! Why, here was a Rubens, no less. And a Corot—or was it? The light was so bad. This Matisse—good, yes, but . . . And the Cézanne. Oh, no. Resoundingly no. Light or no light I would swear that Cézanne never laid a brush to it. A painting was right or it wasn't, and these weren't right. None of them. Let the so-called experts haggle, everyone knew that you had to trust to instinct because ninety-nine times out of a hundred the first gut reaction about a picture was the right one.

The Monet did it. I knew what it was because it was famous, one of the first fakes unmasked in the Sidney Muss masterpiece scandal. And I knew where I was, all right. I was in the middle of Muss's Folly. Marvin Greenspan's information was correct. They hadn't been destroyed. And they were here in this room.

In the center stood a large studio easel. Sitting on it was a "Renoir" landscape. The only light in the room—a Tensor lamp on the adjacent work table—was focused on the canvas, which swam with sensuous greens and blues. The work table itself was a shambles of materials—oils and glazes and dry pigments and tubes and jars and brushes and rags. I had never seen such an array. Name a color and it was there, as were all the oils—olive, linseed, nut, sun-dried poppy—and all the tools—a big flashlight for "raking" surfaces, a magnifier for close work, a sculptor's spatula, pliers, corks, open jars of solution of ammonia, turpentine and spirit varnish . . .

There was an exhibition catalogue lying open on the corner of the table nearest the easel. It was open to a full-color plate of a Renoir listed as part of an exhibition of the early Muss collection. It was the same as the Renoir on the easel but with subtle differences. The easel picture was in the process of being "doctored." I was in a forger's studio and, just as Greenspan had intimated in his letter, changes were being made to the "first bum cargo" so that the paintings could be unloaded. Muss could have the satisfaction of finding collectors whose gullibility would make him forget his own.

They were being changed just enough so they wouldn't be recognized as the famous Muss fakes and just enough so they could be sold elsewhere as "originals." It was wild, yet definitely ingenious and just mad enough to work. Yes, that was it. All over the world these paintings would be channeled into the underground art market as the originals of themselves—the original masterpieces from which the Muss "fakes" had been copied!

I stepped back for a better look at the painting on the easel. This forger, whoever he was, was good—a modern-day Van Meegeren.

In stepping back I was carried into the shadows of the room, where I noticed for the first time the bulk of a chair in the darkness. Then, as my eyes became adjusted, I saw that it was occupied. A man was sitting there with his arms dangling. He was looking straight at me, but he didn't speak or move.

And there was a bullet hole drilled tidily in almost the exact center of his forehead.

Before last summer I would have done something stupid—cried out or fainted or something. But so much had happened. I was tougher now.

And I knew who he was. I recognized him. That helped keep me steady.

You should have stayed in Paris, I thought. You are out of your league here. I even felt a little pity.

I couldn't stop looking. His last expression hadn't quite had time to fade from his face. I tried to fathom it. Was it disbelief? Resentment? Terror? He must have been standing and retreated, slowly, until he stumbled against the chair and sank into it and died there. Watching the bullet on its way.

196

There was a paintbrush lying at his feet, three soft spots of green paint spattered on the floor. That green—we used to call it "Gainsborough green," it was so much his special shade. It was his favorite color, too, for hiding his signature in among the grasses of his best landscapes.

Beyond the paint spots on the floor were more canvases. These were not yet on stretchers and they were laid out flat in neat rows.

It was a physical effort to move past the body in the chair. I kept one eye turned in my head to watch him even though I realized that it was an absurd precaution. I bent over. There on the floor, face up to let their brand-new signatures dry, were the seventeen paintings that were supposed to have been discovered last night at Gregor's dinner party. Seventeen paintings someone had been fast enough and clever enough to remove when Roberts, who would certainly deny it, slipped off for a smoke or a drink.

The voice almost made me jump out of my skin. For one vein-severing instant I was sure the dead man in the chair had spoken. But it was all right. When I turned my head stiffly I saw that it was Oliver, and what he was saying was perfectly ordinary under the circumstances and not frightening at all.

"God Almighty, Persis, what's all this?"

All my new-found character went up in smoke. It must have been a combination of shock and relief. Anyway, my insides began turning over and over, and I stumbled to the work table and doubled over, gasping with nausea and fighting for control. Bang! My head went down on the surface and I stayed that way, bent over in the most inglorious position and drenched in my own cold perspiration. Fumes from uncapped bottles swirled around me.

"Where's the gun, Persis?" He sounded so far away.

"Uh—gun?" I hadn't seen any gun.

He didn't ask again. "Any idea who he is? Was?"

"Jules Toussant, a forger. He was the one following me."

"Well, I was following you, too. Knew you'd get into trouble sooner or later." His voice seemed to be moving around the room by itself, coming to me from here and there with different intensities. "I see. Yes, I see." He would have seen, instantly. After all, he had exposed the fakes in the first place. "So Muss was going to fix his forgeries up and sell them, was he?"

I straightened up slowly. "And look over here on the floor. He was forging Gainsborough Brown signatures, too."

"Jesus! I don't believe it! Not bad, either!"

We looked at each other.

"Persis," he said finally. "We notify the police. Right now."

He was right. No proof needed—here was a genuine, grade-A murder, and no one could deny it. There was no question of an accident this time. They would have to listen.

"I suppose there's a telephone somewhere," he said.

"I suppose back there in the bedroom. Or . . ."—I looked at the windows of the north wall— "probably over here somewhere where you could talk and look out over the Sound at the same time." I walked over but there weren't any tables or furniture for a telephone to be on.

Oliver was starting back toward the bedroom.

I didn't find a telephone. But I noticed something else— small cubes glued to the windows. I knew what they were, all right. Sensors. We had them in our alarm system at the gallery. There was probably a panic button here, too. But no phone. I turned around to tell Oliver, and I couldn't believe what I saw. There he was, just going out of the room, only he wasn't going out of the room: He was folding up in slow motion, the entire length of him buckling and toppling over like a felled tree.

Then I saw her, where he had been, and the glint of the silver medallion on the gun she had used to club him down. Oliver's Colt Thirty-eight. It had to be.

———————

My first reaction was simple idiot surprise at how completely I'd been fooled.

She was wrapped in one of those European-style trenchcoats—very mannish with lots of buckles and straps and buttons. Her hands were gloved; one of them held Oliver's revolver. She'd stolen it from the drawer in my desk while she was playing invalid at my house. That much was obvious.

"Put that down, please. I've gone to too much bloody trouble over those paintings to have one of them ruined now." She was waving the gun at me. I hadn't realized until that moment that I was holding a Gainsborough Brown in my hand. I must have picked it up when I was showing Oliver the signature.

"Alida!" It just wasn't possible.

"Dear Persis," she said mockingly. "You had better believe me when I say that nothing is going to stop me now, and I advise you to just set that painting down as carefully as you can, and as quickly." I couldn't help but admire her coolness.

Would I ever have guessed? I wondered. She and Toussant had confused the issue so prettily on so many points: Gainsborough's wooden box that was actually just so many red herrings, planted in my house so Toussant could search without betraying his real objective, the "insurance" paintings; Alida's phobia about doors and windows, designed to keep anyone from suspecting the Frenchman's nightly pilgrimage up the outside stairs to Alida's bedroom to consult with his mistress; Toussant's discovery of the "murder" drawing from my sketchbook and the decision for me to have a fatal accident on Alida's balcony, and Toussant's forgery of the false certificate that persuaded Gains that Alida was Lydia Wentworth's daughter, then his arrival in America as Alida's chauffeur, and his having to decamp when Gains found out the birth certificate he sold him was a phony.

"You, you never tried to commit suicide! You worked it so you'd be discovered in time. You just wanted to get into my house. You were never really ill." My fingers tightened on the painting. I knew that the minute I put it down I was dead. Keep it between you and her, I told myself wildly. She'll never put a hole in it! Not after all this.

She was touching Oliver lightly with the toe of her shoe, in just the way one might prod a dead animal. "He shouldn't have come here and gotten into all of this. Too bad. He was rather an important person."

I was surprised at the anger that flashed through me when all I should have been feeling was fear. "Every person is important, every living being is important. What about Gainsborough Brown? He was important and you killed him, didn't you? And Eleanore de Pauw?"

"Oh, well, what would you have me do? Eleanore saw me pick up Susan's cloak. She was on the lookout for that foolish husband of hers. I needed it to wear because I knew what I was going to do if he wouldn't listen to reason. Then, if anyone saw me, they'd think I was one of the actors." She shrugged. "You say Gains was important? When I first met Gains I thought he was rich, too, as well as important. He was certainly throwing money around. What did you expect me to do? I *had* to get out of the life I was in—boring, penny-pinching, unbearable. Then he was always talking about Lydia Wentworth. So I had Toussant make up those papers. And Gains—he was such a fool—he believed in them." She shook her head angrily, impatient at the memory. The gun wobbled in her hand, then steadied. "I never dreamed he'd go right off and try to blackmail her. I thought he'd at least wait until she died and then try to claim her estate, and by then I would have figured out something." Her tone implied that her husband hadn't been very considerate.

"But he must have been wild when he found out it was a lie," I said. Keep her talking, that was the thing. And don't let go of the painting.

"He left me black and blue, that's all." Her eyes narrowed. "And he told me I'd have to get out the minute Lydia Wentworth's party was over. I could stay until then for appearances' sake, but after that I had to get out." She paused. "So I killed him. What else could I do?"

200

I could think of a number of things she could have done, but the woman standing coolly over Oliver would never have considered any of the alternatives I had to suggest.

How blind I've been, I thought helplessly. Of all the people in the world, I should have been the one to recognize that Alida was play-acting at being sick. Even with my artist's eye I was taken in by her performance.

"This works out well," she was saying. "They'll find you at Sidney Muss's house—no connection with me at all. I was pleased when Toussant had a chance to do some 'conservation' work for Muss, and Muss set him up here to work on his fakes. It does shift the emphasis nicely."

"I suppose Toussant had a transatlantic reputation?" I was talking to kill time.

"Certainly. He was a man of special talents." She made a gesture with the gun. "If you'll be good enough to put that painting down at once."

"How did you know these paintings existed?" I asked, still stalling.

"Gains told me. Bragged that he'd hidden some un-signed pictures from Gregor. I was always pretty sure that if anyone knew where they were it would be you. He trusted you. You were the only one he might have told. That's why we let you live after the balcony accident failed."

"He never told me." She wouldn't believe me, but it didn't matter.

"The painting," she reminded me.

My hand slid along the work table behind me, searching. Not ten minutes ago I'd had my head on that table, down among all those familiar fumes. Now, if I could trust my memory—and my touch—if I could keep from any obvious motion that would alert her . . .

"Before you shoot that thing, Alida, there are one or two things you ought to know about these paintings."

"Yes?" No expression.

"To begin with, you might be interested to know that Gainsborough Brown never painted a picture in his life. He

201

was the biggest hoax in the history of art. His wife painted them all."

She didn't believe me, but she was listening. "What wife?"

"His only wife." My fingers stopped their search. This should be the right jar. I glanced down at Oliver. For one small second I had the impression that he was stirring. I may have imagined it, but there was no time to look. "Hope Ives. Still his wife. The only one he ever had. Didn't you know? He never divorced her. Nothing belongs to you. Not his name. Not his house. Not his fame. Not these paintings. Nothing." For emphasis, I risked a childish taunt, "You're nobody and nothing."

And while she was temporarily confused, trying to grasp what I'd said, I threw the ammonia at her, momentarily filling the space between us and drenching her face.

The rest was chaos. Oliver suddenly got to his feet and began to struggle with her. Alida fought back like a tigress. And I was screaming over and over again, "Murderess . . . murderess . . . murderess . . . bitch . . . bitch . . . bitch . . ."

Finally Oliver sagged against the wall, holding the back of his head, his foot triumphantly on the gun. She ran, then, out of the greenhouse and down the drive toward the staff's garage. Her car was found there later, parked next to Toussant's. I ran out after her, but I couldn't see her because the fog was in now. I listened for the sound of her running feet, but what I heard instead was a sudden shriek of brakes slicing the fog. A second's silence. Then the hollow thunk of a car's doors banging.

"Never had a chance to stop. She ran right out." A bewildered defensive man's voice.

Oliver had caught up with me finally. "What was that?" He was not quite steady.

"That was the police," I said. "They were coming up here a hundred miles an hour with their lights off, wanting to catch burglars in the act. You see, I called them."

"What?" We were whispering. I could hear the police calling for an ambulance on their radio.

"When I couldn't find a phone, I decided the quickest way to get the police was to activate the alarm system. I was just going to tell you what I had done when Alida smashed you."

"But the alarm was off."

"Yes. But there was a panic button. Right near the studio windows. I knew it would call the police just like the regular alarm does. Just like at the gallery."

"Well, for God's sake, Persis! Let's get out of here!" he said in a iouder voice.

The fourth stage of Gainsborough Brown was over.

The waves made drumming sounds on the beach sixty feet below where I lay on the partially enclosed terrace. Far off to the right I saw the pink bus from the Castle Harbor Hotel snaking its way through the dunes to discharge a load of swimmers. Below, on Aunt Lydie's own expanse of beach, two dogs raced back and forth on the sand, dividing their energies between frenzied digging for the white, sideways-running crabs and short forays into the sea. I'd watched them every morning all week; I suppose they came from one of the several houses that clutched the sides of the cliffs of Tuckerstown. Right now the big one, a German shepherd, was up to his neck in water, snapping at a school of fish. With his pointed ears and pointed jaws, he looked exactly like a scissors. A scissors dog, I thought, smiling.

Somewhere, in faraway New York, the horror was still going on. Press, radio, television ... the whole thing. Snatches appeared in *The Royal Gazette,* but only snatches. Here in Bermuda I was wonderfully remote, protected on all sides by the walls of Lydia Wentworth's seventeen-room "cottage" and by the well-bred reserve of a British-oriented press.

She had been marvelous, Aunt Lydie, calling to offer this house minutes after the story broke. She herself had headed for Paris on the first flight, correctly anticipating the orgy of publicity that would follow the discovery of the unlovely death of Alida Brown beneath the wheels of a car.

She'd called just yesterday from Paris to report that it was freezing there and that she was sure she was getting a cold, although she really didn't have time for one because Gérard du Prey was keeping her busy consoling him on the death of his daughter.

"He's taking it quite well, however, especially since she turned out to be such a heroine, tracking down that forger and shooting him for forging Gainsborough's signature. Gérard says she *had* to kill him. It was the only honorable thing to do. So very French, you know. All France is proud of her. She's become a national figure."

I wondered how much Gérard had guessed of the truth and if he was as grateful as I was for the simple conclusions the authorities had drawn when the box of shells in her pocket connected Alida to the gun and to the dead Toussant and to the Gainsborough Browns at his feet. It never occurred to them that there was any other explanation. Oliver and I had given short, unsensational statements.

"Oliver's coming," my aunt had said yesterday, finally getting to the point of her call. "I told him he had my permission. You know, you might think about marriage again, Persis, as I've mentioned before." There was a pause—only a short one because long-distance pauses are expensive. "I would consider it a favor, so I can stop worrying about you."

He should be here almost any moment now. I could see the maid moving around the outside dining room, a dark shadow in the sunlight. She was singing to herself.

I smiled again and turned slightly on the blue canvas lounge in order to let the sun toast my other side. There was practically nothing I wouldn't do for Lydia Wentworth. But marriage? And what did Oliver think of it? Perhaps he had changed his mind after what I had put him through.

Meanwhile, the heat was making me drowsy. There was plenty of time to think about such serious things, I decided. The next stage of Persis Willum was about to begin.

204